Growing Love

Brianna Owczarzak

Copyright © 2020 Brianna Owczarzak

All rights reserved.

ISBN: 9798567085110

DEDICATION

To those brave enough to lose sight of the shore.

ACKNOWLEDGMENTS

To the fans of *Tangled Love*, your love and enthusiasm of the story and characters was so inspiring. When I finished writing the first book, I left it open so there could be a sequel if the demand were there. I was not expecting the amount of positive feedback I had received so quickly. I immediately started writing the sequel for you all. Your love for this story kept me motivated to see it through to the end. I hope you all enjoy it as much as you enjoyed the first book. Thank you so much for your continued support.

To my wonderful friends Amanda, David and Whitney, once again I entrusted you with an advanced copy of this book for your advice and feedback. And you did not disappoint. Your suggestions helped shape this story. I am so thankful for your support and friendship. I love you all.

PROLOGUE

"Marry me," he said.

"What?" Sarah asked surprised.

"Marry me," Charlie said again.

"Charlie, you don't have to do that," she said.

"I know I don't have to. I want to. I've always wanted to," he said.

Sarah looked at Charlie seriously. He pushed his chair back and got down on one knee. He placed her hand in both of his.

"Sarah Simmons, I have loved you from the day I first laid eyes on you. You are my best friend, my confidant, and quite frankly, the best lover I have ever had. Will you make me the happiest man on earth and be my wife?" he asked.

Sarah examined his face. His forest green eyes stared at her softly. She looked down toward her growing baby bump. Then she looked back at Charlie's face. She smiled at him.

"I will," she said.

Charlie was ecstatic. He always wanted to marry Sarah, and now she was going to be his wife. And now he could make good on his promise to Eddie, he thought to himself. He lifted Sarah's hands to his lips and kissed them softly. He moved his lips to her belly and kissed that too.

"I already love you," he whispered to her stomach.

Sarah wiped a tear from her eye. She knew she was making the right decision. Charlie was going to be a great dad to their baby, she thought. She also knew Charlie would do anything to make her happy. She could be happy enough with Charlie, she decided.

She still had feelings for Tim though, and she knew those feelings weren't just going to go away. But she had a baby on the way. She couldn't just think about herself anymore. She had to make the best decisions for her growing baby and right now, that was Charlie.

"What are you thinking about?" he asked, examining her face.

"How right this feels," she answered.

Charlie smiled at her. He got off his knee and kissed Sarah softly on the lips. She smiled up at him.

"I do love you, Charlie," she said.

"I know," he replied.

1

The next morning, Charlie wasn't at the hospital. He didn't want to be there when Tim showed up. He knew that was a conversation that needed to take place without him. Even though Charlie was getting what he wanted, he found himself questioning the scenario. He knew things wouldn't have worked out the way they did if it wasn't for Sarah's current condition.

He wondered what life would be like if Sarah didn't get in that accident. He questioned if she would have told him she was pregnant with their baby. He wondered if she would have kept it or if she would have convinced Tim it was his. He couldn't see Sarah doing that. She would have told him, and they would have ended up together, he decided.

Instead of worrying about the issue further, Charlie went shopping for an engagement ring for Sarah. He went to a handful of different stores before he found the perfect ring. It was a slim white gold band with a single round diamond in the center. It was simple, yet classic. He knew Sarah would love it. She was never a fan of over-the-top rings. She once told him love should be measured by the heart, not the size of the diamond. He couldn't believe he remembered that.

He was going to surprise Sarah with the ring later that evening. Their plan was to get married that week so Sarah could get put on Charlie's health insurance and continue receiving the treatments she needed to fully recover. The ceremony wasn't going to be anything spectacular because it was on short notice and had to take place in the hospital. But Charlie wanted it to be as perfect as possible. In his head, he planned to have Sarah's dream wedding at a later date after she was in better shape physically and mentally.

He pictured her walking down the aisle toward him in a beautiful white dress. But of course, the dress wouldn't be half as beautiful as she is, he thought. His heart broke a little when he realized Eddie wouldn't be there to walk her down the aisle. He missed Eddie. He made a mental note to go visit the cemetery that week.

Meanwhile, back at the hospital, Tim brought Sarah a bouquet of calla lilies. She was pleasantly surprised because she never shared the meaning of the flower with him. He usually brought her roses. Charlie must have mentioned it to him, she thought.

"They're beautiful," she said as Tim placed the vase by the window in her hospital room.

"How are you feeling today?" he asked as he turned around and made his way toward her bed.

He sat down in one of the chairs adjacent to the bed and grabbed one of Sarah's hands.

"I'm doing OK," she said smiling at him.

She liked Tim. Everything was always easy with him. He was laid back and always down for whatever. She was going to miss that. She was going to miss him. She hoped they would remain friends, but that probably wouldn't be easy. She knew she had to tell him about Charlie, but she didn't want to. She didn't want things to be over between them.

Sarah looked down at her growing belly and knew she couldn't think that way anymore. She had to think about her baby and what was best for him/her. She needed health insurance to make sure both her and the baby were healthy. Charlie could and was willing to give her that. She looked back at Tim.

"I need to tell you something," she said.

"I need to tell you something too," he said.

Sarah looked at him quizzically. He looked at her hand and lightly stroked it with his thumb. Then he looked back at her face. She was beautiful, even without makeup, he thought.

"I love you, Sarah," Tim said.

Sarah was taken aback. She was not expecting that. She and Tim had only dated for two months before she got in the car accident. Then she was in a coma for about a month. She liked Tim, but she wasn't ready to say those words to him. It was too soon, she thought. Tim read her face.

"I was going to tell you that when we went away for the weekend, but I never got the chance because of the crash," he said.

"Oh," Sarah said, processing the information.

"It's OK. You don't have to say it back. I just wanted you to know," he said.

She was quiet for a minute as she formulated the words in her head.

"I like you, Tim. I really do. But I can't say those words to you," she said.

"That's OK," he said. "I'll still be here when you're ready."

"I won't ever be able to say those words to you," she said slowly.

Tim looked at her confused.

"I don't understand," he said.

"Charlie and I are getting married. He proposed to me last night," Sarah said.

"What?" Tim asked shockingly.

"I need health insurance and I can get put on Charlie's insurance if we get married," she explained.

"If that's why you're doing it, then we can find another way," he said.

"That's not the only reason," she said, looking at her stomach.

"Is this because of the baby?" Tim asked.

Sarah could sense he was becoming angry. His voice was getting louder.

"It's his baby," she said.

"That doesn't matter. You don't have to keep it, Sarah. This wasn't part of your plan. There's no shame in getting rid of it. None of us will judge you," he said.

Now Sarah was becoming angry. She couldn't imagine getting an abortion now. Even though she was only a few months along, she loved her baby. She felt a connection to it that she couldn't explain.

"I'm not getting rid of it, Tim," she said defensively.

"OK, well we can figure it out then. You don't have to marry him," Tim said.

"I know I don't have to. But I am. This was my choice," Sarah said.

He was silent. He released Sarah's hand and stared at her.

"Why are you doing this?" he asked after a moment.

"Because it's the right thing to do," she replied.

"Forget what's right, Sarah. Do what's going to make you happy," Tim said.

That last word lingered in her head. Happy. It's what Edward wrote to her in his last letter. *I just want you to be happy*, the letter read. She could see herself being happy with Charlie and Tim. But things were still new with Tim. She didn't know him as well as she knew Charlie. She knew all of Charlie's secrets and bad habits, and they didn't scare her.

"This will make me happy," Sarah said convincingly.

Tim examined her face closely. Then his face hardened.

"Would you have went back to him if you didn't get in that crash?" he asked.

Sarah paused while thinking about that question.

"I don't know," she answered honestly.

"Fuck, Sarah. This isn't how things are supposed to be. Things were going so good between us," he said.

"I know, but life is funny that way," she said. "Sometimes it takes a tragedy to make you realize what's important."

"Are you saying I'm not important to you?" Tim asked.

"That's not what I meant," she replied.

"That's exactly what it sounded like," he said.

"Tim, that's not what I meant. All I meant was I have a baby on the way. I'm going to be a mother," she said, pondering that last word.

She was going to be a mother, she realized. She knew she was going to be a mom but saying it out loud made it seem more real. Sarah moved her hand to her stomach and rested it there.

"And that's more important than anything else right now," she said.

"That's more important than your own happiness?" Tim asked.

"I'm going to be happy, Tim. This baby is all I need. And Charlie is going to be a great dad to him or her," Sarah said.

"I understand that, and I'm sure he will be. But what about you?" he asked.

"I'm going to be just fine," she said matter-of-factly.

"I hope so, Sarah," Tim said.

They stared at each other in silence for a moment. Neither of them wanted to speak because they knew it was over between them. Their summer of passion had come to an end in a way neither of them could have predicted. Sarah knew Tim could never accept her child and she couldn't expect him to. She never gave him a chance to try, but his words confirmed her belief, she thought to herself.

"Well, I guess I should go," he finally said.

Sarah looked at him with a half-smile. Tim grabbed her hand one more time.

"Goodbye, Sarah," he said.

"Goodbye, Tim," she replied.

Tim released her hand, nodded to himself, and walked out of the hospital room. Sarah thought she would cry, but she didn't. She looked down at her stomach and knew she made the right decision for her growing family, and that gave her a sense of comfort she hadn't felt in a long time.

She used that feeling to doze off to sleep. She awoke about two hours later to Charlie sitting next to her bed. He was watching TV and didn't notice she had woken up. Sarah used her unbroken arm to sit herself up. That movement caught Charlie's attention.

"Hello, fiancé," he said, smiling at her.

"Hello," she said, smiling back.

She repeated the word fiancé in her head. She liked the way that sounded slipping off of Charlie's tongue. She couldn't believe she was going to be a wife in a few days. She was going to be Charlie's wife. It was something the two of them had dreamed about when they were little kids, and now it was becoming a reality.

"I got you something," he said.

"You did?" she asked.

"I did," he said smiling.

Charlie pulled a small ring box out of his pocket. Sarah's eyes widened. He opened it up and pulled the ring out. She extended her left hand so he could place it on her ring finger. After he did, she spread her fingers apart so she could examine it.

"It's perfect," she said.

"Just like you," Charlie replied.

"Thank you, Charlie," she said smiling.

"You're welcome, Sare-bear," he said.

Charlie leaned forward and gave Sarah a light kiss on the lips. She moved her left hand behind his neck and held him there. She slowly slid her tongue into his mouth before quickly retracting it back into hers. Then she smiled up at him.

"I've missed your kisses," he said.

"Well, you're going to be getting a lot of them, fiancé," she replied.

"I better be," he said, giving her a wink.

2

A few days later was Wednesday, Sept. 3. It was the day Charlie and Sarah were getting married. One of the nurses had wheeled Sarah's bed to a separate location in the hospital so she could get ready for the big day without Charlie seeing her. This allowed Charlie and Susan to decorate Sarah's hospital room for the occasion without her noticing.

They strung twinkle lights across the ceiling, and even made a makeshift altar around where Sarah's bed would be. They sprinkled flower petals across the floor to form an aisle. Sarah's right arm and leg were still in casts from the crash, so she was not able to walk down the aisle. Instead, one of her nurses was going to wheel her bed into the room at the right moment.

"It looks pretty good," Susan said after she and Charlie finished decorating.

"It does, doesn't it?" Charlie asked.

Susan nodded at him.

"I'm going to go check on your bride. I'll see you at the ceremony," she said.

Charlie smiled and Susan left the room. It was going to be a small ceremony with Charlie's parents and Susan as witnesses. The hospital had an ordained minister that was going to officiate it. It wasn't anything like what Charlie had imagined the day would be, but he was still excited. He had waited most of his life to make Sarah his wife, and now it was happening. He rented a black tuxedo for the special occasion.

Charlie didn't know it, but Susan had picked out a white dress for Sarah to wear. She also arranged for a hairstylist and makeup artist to come to the hospital to make Sarah look extra special. Sarah was Susan's only niece, and she wanted this day to be as perfect as possible for her. She only wished her brother were still alive to witness it.

"I know your dad is looking down to be here today," Susan said.

Sarah just smiled at her aunt. She didn't believe in Heaven, but it was a nice thought. She always pictured her dad walking her down the aisle when she planned her wedding in her head. Sometimes she pictured herself marrying Charlie. Other times it was to a hot celebrity, like Zac Efron. Sarah was sad her dad wasn't alive to walk her down the aisle, but she knew there wasn't anybody else her dad would rather her marry. She knew she was making him proud.

The circumstances weren't perfect and just a few days prior, she was someone else's girlfriend. But she and Charlie were having a baby together and that was the only thing that mattered to her. She didn't even think about Tim that day. In fact, for the first time since getting engaged, Sarah was actually looking forward to getting married.

"Are you ready?" Susan asked.

"I am," Sarah responded.

"OK, I'll see you in there," Susan replied.

Susan left Sarah with the nurse and made her way into the hospital room. Charlie was standing up at the altar in a black tuxedo. Underneath, he was wearing a white vest and a white bowtie. His parents were standing off to the side. Susan went and stood next to them.

A few moments later, "Marry You" by Bruno Mars started playing over the speaker in the room. Charlie could hear the wheels on Sarah's bed getting closer. He had butterflies in his stomach. Sarah's bed entered the room and Charlie saw his bride for the first time that day. She was wearing a long white lace A-line style dress that hung off her shoulders. It gave him flashbacks to their senior prom.

He smiled so big as happy tears flowed down his face. He didn't even bother to wipe them away. That moment was the happiest he had ever been in his life. He had never felt joy as pure as he did when he saw Sarah in her wedding dress. Seeing Charlie cry, made Sarah tear up. She laughed and quickly wiped the tears away before it ruined her makeup. The nurse wheeled Sarah's bed up toward Charlie and he grabbed Sarah's hands.

"I love you, Sare-bear," he mouthed to her.

"I love you too," she mouthed back.

For a brief moment, it was just the two of them. Charlie had forgotten there were other people in the room. Then the minister started speaking as the ceremony began, bringing Charlie back to the present.

He smiled at Sarah before turning toward the minister.

"We are gathered here today as Charlie Canton and Sarah Simmons join together in marriage," the minister said.

Sarah gave Charlie's hand a light squeeze and he smiled at her. She smiled back. She truly looked happy, he thought to himself. Which in return, made him happy. He had his doubts on why Sarah was marrying him, but seeing her in that moment erased all of that uncertainty he had felt.

The minister gave a brief synopsis of what marriage means and then went into the vows. Charlie and Sarah opted for the traditional wedding vows instead of writing their own. In Charlie's head, they would deliver personal vows at a later ceremony once Sarah was fully recovered. He hadn't shared any of those ideas with her, but that was his plan.

"I do," Charlie said, after the minister finished reading the vows to him.

The minister repeated the same vows to Sarah. Charlie's butterflies returned as he examined her face. He didn't think she would say no, but a slight feeling of uncertainty had returned. Sarah gave him a wink.

"I do," she said.

Charlie let out a slight sigh of relief and smiled at her. She smiled back. He could hear his parents and Susan cheering. Even though they were just a few feet away, they sounded far off in the distance. It was just him and Sarah again – until the minister began speaking, bringing him back to the present.

"By the power vested in me by the state of Indiana, I now pronounce you husband and wife. You may kiss the bride," the minister said.

Charlie leaned down and kissed Sarah lightly on the lips. He went to pull away, but she held him there. She slid her tongue into his mouth and then back into hers. She released him, but Charlie went in for another kiss. This time, he slipped his tongue into her mouth and danced it around hers before pulling away. He gave her a big smile before turning toward his parents.

Sarah's heart was racing. After that kiss, she wanted Charlie. She knew that wasn't going to happen with her current condition, and the fact she was still in the hospital, but she wanted him. She caught herself staring in the direction of his manhood and quickly forced her eyes away. She saw his parents walking toward them.

"You look beautiful, Sarah," said Marie, Charlie's mom.

"Thank you, Mrs. Canton," Sarah replied.

"Please, call me mom," Marie responded, leaning over Sarah's bed to give her a hug.

Sarah hugged her back and smiled. *Mom*, Sarah repeated in her head. She had a mom again. She didn't remember what that felt like, but that current moment was a nice feeling.

"OK," Sarah said.

Charlie smiled at her and then at his parents. His dad, Ray, reached his hand out to Charlie. He took it and shook it.

"Thanks for coming," Charlie told his parents.

"We wouldn't miss it for the world," Ray said.

Ray turned his attention to Sarah.

"I'm really happy you're doing well, Sarah. Our boy was a wreck there for a while," he said.

"Dad," Charlie said embarrassed.

"You were," Ray said before turning his attention back to Sarah. "We didn't know if you were going to make it or not. Charlie here, didn't sleep much those few weeks."

Sarah looked up at Charlie and he gave her a half-smile.

"I wasn't going to let you off the hook that easy," she said jokingly.

They all laughed. Then Susan joined the Cantons at the bed.

"I should get going," she said. "You really do look beautiful, Sarah."

"Thanks for everything, Aunt Susan," Sarah responded.

"You're quite welcome, my dear. I'll see you later this week," Susan said. "Bye, Charlie."

"Bye, Susan," he replied.

Susan waved goodbye to the Canton family and left the room. That's when Sarah noticed her nurse and the minister were no longer in the room. She didn't notice they left, but she was OK with it. She couldn't wait to have Charlie all to herself. She turned her attention back to his parents.

"We should get going too," Ray said, giving his son a friendly nudge.

Charlie laughed.

"It was really nice seeing you, Sarah. It has been too long," Marie said.

"I'm sure we'll be seeing a lot more of each other, mom," Sarah said, smiling at her.

Marie smiled back.

"I'm sure we will," she said.

Marie gave her son a hug and grabbed her husband's hand.

"Now, you kids try not to have too much fun tonight," Ray said, winking at the newlyweds.

They both laughed and waved goodbye as Charlie's parents walked out of the room.

"Now, it's just you and me," Charlie said, smiling at his bride.

"What would you like to do?" Sarah asked suggestively.

"I have an idea," he said, grinning at her.

He sat on the edge of her bed and pulled out his phone.

"I would like us to have our first dance," he said.

He began to play Mariah Carey's "We Belong Together." He wrapped his arm around Sarah and swayed with her back and forth. Tears began to fall from her eyes. He wiped them away with his thumb and gave her a light kiss on the lips.

"I love you, so much," he said.

"I love you too, Charlie," she replied.

They held each other for the remainder of the song.

"Are you going to stay with me tonight?" Sarah asked after the song was over.

"You're my wife. I'm going to stay with you every night," Charlie replied.

"Really?" she asked, her eyes lighting up.

"Of course. I'll always be here for you," he said.

Sarah used her left arm to pull him close to her. She lifted her head up toward him and he looked down to her. He lowered his face until their lips met. She slid her tongue inside his mouth and then back into hers. She grabbed his upper lip with hers and pulled on it lightly. Then she thrusted her tongue back into his mouth. Charlie kissed her back aggressively and then quickly pulled away. She looked at him confused.

"Baby, you're making me want you," he said.

"Good. Because I want you too," she said moving her face toward his.

Charlie bit his lip and looked at her.

"We can't," he said.

"Why not?" she asked.

"Well, one, we're in a hospital. Somebody could walk in at any moment. And two, I don't want to hurt you," he said.

Sarah sighed. She knew he was right, but that didn't change her craving.

"Let me check something really quick," Charlie said, getting off the bed.

He walked over to the door and peeked into the hallway. There wasn't anyone out there. He walked back toward Sarah's bed.

"How about we get you out of that dress and into something a little more comfortable. Then I can make you feel good," he said.

Sarah's face lit up and she nodded her head. She leaned forward so Charlie could access the back of the dress. He unbuttoned it all the way and slowly pulled the front down off of her breasts. She wasn't wearing a bra. The sight of her bare breasts made his penis grow. He quickly adjusted himself and continued taking the dress off her. He struggled slightly when the dress reached the cast on her leg, but he managed to get it off.

Charlie hung the dress over the back of one of the chairs. Then he walked over to the supply cupboard in Sarah's room. He opened it up and pulled out a clean hospital gown. He carried it to her bed and Sarah made a face at him.

"What?" he asked.

"That's not very sexy," she replied.

"Babe. You literally look sexy in anything," Charlie said.

Sarah rolled her eyes and smiled at him. Charlie helped her into the gown. Then he went and checked the hallway again.

"All clear," he said with a devilish grin.

Sarah's heart was racing as he walked toward her. She didn't know exactly what was about to happen, but she was ready. It was her wedding night, and she wanted her husband. Her sexy, muscular husband, she thought to herself as she eyed his body.

Charlie stopped halfway to the bed and slowly took off the jacket of his tuxedo. He dropped it on the floor. He swayed his hips back and forth as he unbuttoned the vest. He was doing it as a joke, but Sarah was loving every second of it. He dropped the vest next to the jacket.

He continued to sway his hips as he unbuttoned his dress shirt, which he dropped on the floor as well. He walked toward the bed wearing his dress pants and a white T-shirt. Charlie gave Sarah a wink as he climbed onto the side of her bed. He lifted one of his hands to her chin and kissed her hard on the lips.

He thrusted his tongue inside her mouth and slid it across her tongue. He retreated his tongue back into his mouth and repeated that motion another time. He moved his lips to her neck where he left a trail of kisses up to her ear. He gently grabbed her lower earlobe with his teeth and gave it a light pull. Sarah let out a soft moan.

Charlie went back to kissing her neck as he ran a hand up her inner thigh. Her heart was racing. She hadn't been touched like that in over a month and she was ready. He slid his hand under her gown and up toward her vagina. Her breathing accelerated.

He rubbed his hand back and forth over her underwear until he could feel the wetness soak through the fabric. He slowly pulled her underwear down to her thighs. He moved his hand back up to her vagina as he kissed her on the lips again. He gently flicked her clitoris with his index finger as he moved his hand down to her opening.

He traced his index finger around her hole before thrusting it inside. Sarah grabbed the back of his neck and held his face to hers as she forced her tongue inside his mouth. Charlie moved his finger in and out a few times before combining it with his middle finger. He pushed his two fingers inside of her as far as he could. Sarah pulled her head back and let out a quiet moan.

Charlie thrusted those two fingers inside of her, pushing them harder and faster. Sarah's breathing continued to accelerate. She wanted Charlie. She wanted all of him and his fingers weren't going to cut it.

"I want you," she whispered in his ear.

"I want you, too," he replied. "But in the meantime, you're just going to have to enjoy this."

He smiled at her. She did not smile back. Charlie very rarely told her no for anything, and she did not like it when he did. He continued to move his fingers in and out of her, but she was no longer in the mood. Charlie's rejection had turned her off. She turned her head toward the wall. Charlie slowly pulled his fingers out of her and looked at her.

"Are you OK?" he asked.

"No," she replied.

"What's wrong?" he asked.

"It's our fucking wedding night and I just want you. And I want you to want me. I want to feel sexy instead of some handicapped person who is bedridden," Sarah pouted.

Charlie let out a laugh. Sarah glared at him.

"Baby. I do want you. And you are sexy. Casts and all," he replied.

She raised an eyebrow at him.

"Trust me. I wish I could be all over you right now, but that's just not feasible given the current circumstances. I'm trying my best to make you feel good. Once you're better, we can have all the sex you want," he said smiling.

"All of it?" she asked.

"A lifetime of it," he replied.

Sarah smiled. She liked the sound of that.

"After all, you're my wife now. You're stuck with me 'til death do us part," Charlie said.

"Let's not talk about death," she said as she nuzzled her head against his chest.

Charlie put her underwear back into place and pulled the blanket over them. They fell asleep holding each other as husband and wife.

3

A week after the wedding, Sarah had her back brace removed. The casts on her arm and leg came off a week after that, and she was cleared to go home. She still had several weeks of physical therapy and follow-up appointments, but she was excited to sleep in her own bed again. She had been in the hospital for nearly seven weeks.

Charlie drove the two of them to Sarah's house. He helped her out of the car and supported her as she slowly walked to the front door. She was still getting accustomed to walking again since it had been so long. The hospital gave her a cane to use for support, but Sarah refused to use it. Her self-esteem had taken a beating since the crash and she just wanted to feel normal again.

Once they reached the front door, Charlie stopped. He bent down and picked Sarah up so he was carrying her in his arms.

"What are you doing?" she asked while laughing.

"This is our first time returning home as husband and wife. I have to carry you over the threshold," he replied.

Sarah laughed as he opened the door and carried her inside the house. He placed her feet on the floor slowly and held her to make sure she could balance herself. Once she seemed stable, he let go. Sarah grabbed a hold of the railing heading upstairs for support. She began to look around the house and tried to remember the last time she was there.

It was the night of the crash. She had taken two pregnancy tests in the bathroom upstairs, which confirmed she was pregnant. She was devastated by the news back then. She was angry and confused. She didn't know what to do, so she left. The events that happened after that were a blur.

Sarah was now nearly 13-weeks pregnant and married. She looked at Charlie and couldn't believe he was there with her. She couldn't believe they were actually married. She treated him poorly before the crash. He was there for her and she just didn't appreciate him back then, she thought. She felt bad for the way she treated him, but he was here now and she wasn't going to let that happen again.

"What are you thinking about?" Charlie asked as he examined her face.

"How sorry I am," she said.

He looked at her confused.

"I'm so sorry for the way I treated you, Charlie. I never should have ended things between us. I'm so sorry for all of it. You were so perfect and nice to me and I don't deserve you after what I did," Sarah said.

Charlie pulled her into a hug. She pressed her head against his chest and held him.

"It's OK, baby. That's all in the past. It doesn't matter anymore. What matters is you're here. You're alive. And we're married! And we're growing a family," he said as he moved one of his hands to Sarah's stomach.

She pulled her head back and looked at him.

"You're not mad at me?" she asked.

"No," he responded. "I was. I was furious with you for a while. But then the crash happened, and I didn't care what happened between us. I just wanted you to get better. I didn't care about anything else."

Charlie paused for a moment. A tear started to fall from his eye. Sarah reached up and wiped it away with her hand. She looked at him confused.

"I thought I was going to lose you, Sarah. And I realized I couldn't live without you. Even if you just wanted to be friends, I would have been OK with that as long as you were in my life. But for a while there, it didn't look like you were going to make it. That was the hardest thing I've ever been through," he said.

"But you never gave up on me," she said, smiling at him.

"I never did. I knew you had to pull through. That was the only option," he replied.

Sarah stood on her tiptoes and kissed Charlie lightly on the lips. That touch sent a spark through his body. He hadn't had sex with Sarah in months and he wanted her. He had been patient these past few weeks, but he couldn't wait anymore. He picked her up and carried her upstairs to her bedroom.

"What are you doing?" she asked.

"I want you," he replied as he laid her on the bed.

Sarah wasn't expecting that, but she was ready. She had been wanting Charlie since their wedding night. She missed the feeling of his muscles pressed against her naked body. It had been so long she almost forgot what sex with him was like. She lifted her shirt over her head and dropped it on the floor as she eyed Charlie standing before her.

He was staring at her hungrily. He removed his shirt, revealing his bare chest. Sarah drifted her eyes down his body, admiring his muscles. She could feel herself getting wet. Charlie was the only man whose body alone made her feel that way.

Her eyes moved back up to his. He smiled at her, almost as if he knew what his body was doing to her. He casually took off his belt as he eyed her perky breasts peeking out through her nude bra. They had already grown slightly during her pregnancy. He dropped the belt on the floor next to his shirt and began unbuttoning his pants.

Sarah began to grow impatient. She unbuttoned her jeans and quickly pulled them off her legs. She tossed them aside and leaned back on the bed in a seductive pose. She bit her lower lip at Charlie because she knew he couldn't resist when she did that. He quickly removed his pants and climbed onto the bed.

He made his way over her and up to her lips. He kissed her aggressively as he moved one hand behind her back. He slid his tongue inside her mouth as he unclasped her bra. He removed it from her body and dropped it on the floor next to the rest of her clothes. He grabbed her lower lip with his teeth gently and then released.

Sarah wrapped her arms around his back and pulled him down to her body. She thought about rolling him over and climbing on top of him, but she wasn't confident in the strength of her right leg yet. Instead, she moved her lips to his neck and kissed her way up to his ear. She gave it a light nibble before tracing the outside of it with her tongue. She could feel Charlie's penis growing against her thigh.

He kissed his way down her body, but stopped briefly once he reached her breasts. He popped one of her nipples in his mouth and gave it a light suck. After releasing it, he flicked it with his tongue before continuing his way south. Once he reached her underwear, he didn't remove it right away. Instead, he rubbed his nose up and down against her clitoris between the fabric.

Sarah arched her back. The sensation was becoming too much, and she needed Charlie. He grabbed her underwear with his teeth and pulled it down to her thighs. He used his hand to remove it the rest of the way and then tossed it to the floor. He made his way back to her vagina where he gently flicked her clit with his tongue. Sarah let out a soft moan.

"I need you," she called out.

Charlie ignored her and moved down to her opening. He traced it with his tongue before thrusting it inside of her. He missed the way she tasted. She tasted sweet with just a hint of salt. He could sense Sarah was becoming impatient, but he was enjoying himself. It had been a long time and he wanted to take his time. This was their first time having sex as husband and wife, and he wanted to remember every bit of it.

He moved his tongue up and down while it was inside of her. Sarah moaned again as she grabbed the bedsheets with her hands. Charlie pulled his tongue out and then thrusted it back inside of her hard. He moved it in and out, going faster and faster. Sarah moaned louder.

She couldn't take it anymore. She needed him. She grabbed his arms and pulled him up toward her. He smiled at her.

"Now," she demanded.

Charlie let out a light laugh. He quickly removed his underwear and climbed back on top of Sarah. He guided his erect penis inside her. He felt her wetness surround him, almost wrapping him in a warm blanket. He let out a soft moan as he pushed further inside. Sarah parted her lips as she pushed her head back against the pillow.

"Yes," she called out.

Charlie moved in and out slowly, lubricating his penis against her wetness. After a few motions he began to thrust harder. He grabbed the edge of the mattress for support as he pushed harder and harder into her. Sarah moaned louder. He could feel himself about to climax, but he wanted Sarah to reach completion first, so he held back.

He began to make a grunting noise as he thrusted harder and harder. He could hear his body slamming against her pelvis. Sarah arched her back and her legs trembled. She opened her mouth to let out a moan, but nothing came out. Her whole body went numb. At the same time, Charlie released himself inside of her and collapsed onto her body.

He couldn't move. He was too exhausted. Sarah wrapped her arms around his back and held him against her. She couldn't believe what had just happened. That was the first time Charlie had ever made her orgasm.

She didn't know if it was because it had been so long since she had any action or if it was something about being married to him that made her feel a stronger connection to him. Or perhaps he had some practice with another woman while she was with Tim, she thought. That thought made her sad. She didn't want to picture him with anyone else. But she knew it was likely.

Charlie was an attractive man, and she knew the way girls looked at him when they were out in public. Even through his clothes his muscles were observant. Although, it wasn't just his muscles that made him attractive. He had good hair, which he knew how to style, and a chiseled jawline. Ever since high school, Sarah always thought he was model material. She realized Charlie had said something, bringing her back to the present.

"What?" she asked.

"I said I love you," Charlie replied, lifting his head up to look at her.

"I love you, too," she said, smiling at him.

Charlie leaned his face forward and gave her a light kiss on the lips. She returned the kiss and pulled him close to her again.

"I'm never letting you go," she said.

"Good," he responded.

He nuzzled his head against her breasts and closed his eyes. Sarah rubbed her fingers through his hair. She wanted to know if he had hooked up with anyone while they were apart, but she didn't want to ruin the nice moment they were having. She knew she was being selfish about it because she had been hooking up with someone else, but she couldn't help it. Charlie had always been hers, even when he wasn't.

"What are you thinking about?" he asked.

Sarah paused. Now was her chance. She thought about how she wanted to word the question or if she wanted to ask it at all. Maybe ignorance really was bliss, she thought. Her silence caused Charlie to look at her. His face grew concerned.

"What is it, babe?" he asked.

"Did you sleep with anyone while we weren't together?" she asked.

Charlie laughed.

"That's what you're thinking about right now?" he asked.

"I'm curious," she replied.

"No, I didn't," he responded. "Every time I took a girl back to my place, I couldn't go through with it. She wasn't you and I didn't want anyone else."

"Oh," Sarah said, processing that information.

So there were girls, multiple, she thought. She didn't know how she felt about that.

"Can you say the same thing?" Charlie asked, already knowing the answer.

Sarah looked away. She knew she couldn't be upset with Charlie for whatever happened while they were apart because she had been sleeping with Tim.

"You don't have to answer that. I already know the answer," Charlie said sadly.

"Charlie," Sarah said in a consoling tone.

"It's OK. It's in the past. It doesn't matter anymore. All that matters is us, right now. You and me," he said.

"And our baby," she said, moving a hand to her stomach.

Charlie rolled to his side and placed a hand over Sarah's.

"And our baby," he said smiling.

Sarah rolled to her side to face him.

"I love you so much," she said.

"I love you, too," he said with a grin.

"I really do," she said, trying to convince herself more than anything.

"I know," he replied.

He leaned forward and kissed her on the lips. He let his lips linger there for a few moments before pulling them away.

"I will never grow tired of kissing you, Mrs. Canton," he said.

"Good," she said smiling.

"I still can't believe you're my fucking wife," he said, pulling her close. "This is awesome."

Sarah let out a laugh as she snuggled up against her husband.

"Well, start believing it, mister. Because you're stuck with me now," she replied.

4

The next morning, Sarah woke up to a small pool of blood between her legs. She immediately started panicking and shook Charlie to wake him up. He mumbled something and went back to sleep. Sarah stumbled to the bathroom to see if she was still bleeding, but she wasn't. The bleeding had stopped.

The stain on the bed was about the circumference of a tennis ball. It wasn't much, but it was enough to cause Sarah to worry. She began to sob uncontrollably while yelling at Charlie to wake up. He slowly opened his eyes and looked at her. Once he saw she was crying, he jumped out of bed and ran to her.

"Baby, what's wrong?" he asked.

She couldn't form any words. Instead, she pointed at the stain on the bed. Charlie turned to see what she was pointing at. He saw the blood and turned back toward Sarah.

"Is that blood?" he asked concerned.

She nodded her head yes. Sarah placed her hands on her stomach and looked down. Tears continued to pour down her face.

"Babe," Charlie said in a consoling tone as he wrapped his arms around her.

Sarah hugged him and cried into his shoulder.

"We need to get you to the hospital," he said.

"OK," she replied.

She pulled away from the hug and wiped her tears on the back of her hand.

"Do you want to change or do you just want to go?" Charlie asked.

She looked down at her pajamas, which were also stained with blood.

"Can I shower first?" she asked.

"Whatever you want," he replied.

"Will you help me?" she asked.

She realized she hadn't showered by herself since before the crash. She was afraid she might slip and reinjure herself.

"Of course," Charlie said.

The two of them walked to the bathroom and got undressed. Charlie couldn't help but check out Sarah's body as he helped her into the shower. He felt his penis grow slightly as he had flashbacks of their previous shower sex. He pushed the dirty images out of his head as he turned the water on. He gently held Sarah's hips as she cleaned herself. Once she was done, he quickly washed up. Then he helped her out of the shower and they both dried off.

After getting dressed, Charlie threw the sheets in the washer while Sarah got ready. He returned upstairs to find her standing in front of her mirror, staring at her stomach. Her jeans were unbuttoned, and she wasn't wearing a shirt. Charlie moved behind her, wrapped his arms around her and placed his hands on her stomach.

"Are you almost ready?" he asked.

"None of my clothes fit," she replied.

"We can get you new ones," Charlie responded. "In the meantime, do you want to wear one of my shirts?"

Sarah nodded her head yes. Charlie went to his bag – he hadn't fully moved in yet - and pulled out a T-shirt for her to wear. Sarah went to grab it, but he placed it over her head instead. She put her arms through the holes and Charlie pulled it down over her body. It was baggy on her, but it covered her jeans so no one would notice they weren't buttoned.

"You look gorgeous," Charlie said as he pulled her into a hug.

She let out a slight snicker as she pulled away.

"I'm ready," she said somberly.

"OK, let's go," he said as he reached for her hand.

The drive to the hospital was quiet. Charlie couldn't help but think this was his fault. It was all because they had sex last night, he thought to himself. If only he resisted his urges, this never would have happened, he decided. If Sarah lost the baby because of him, he would never forgive himself, he thought.

Meanwhile, Sarah was trying not to think about it. She knew miscarriages were common in the first trimester, but she was almost starting her second trimester. She thought she was safe. She loved her baby, and she didn't want to lose it. She didn't want to come to that conclusion until she knew for sure. She turned the radio up in an attempt to drown out her thoughts.

Charlie glanced at her. He tried to read her expression, but he had no idea what she was thinking. He wondered if she was blaming him too. He felt guilty and he didn't know what to do to make that guilt go away.

A short while later, they arrived at the hospital. Charlie parked the car and then helped Sarah out of the passenger side. They held hands as they entered the emergency room entrance and walked up to the check-in desk.

"How may I help you?" the receptionist asked.

"My wife is pregnant, and we woke up to a decent amount of blood down there this morning," Charlie replied.

Sarah squeezed his hand as a non-verbal thank you. She appreciated him taking the lead because she couldn't bring herself to talk about it. The thought of anything being wrong with her baby made her emotional.

"How far along are you, sweetie?" the receptionist asked.

"Twelve weeks. Twelve-and-a-half weeks," Sarah replied.

"Well, let me get you checked in and someone will be with you shortly," the receptionist responded.

Sarah handed the woman her driver's license and Charlie gave her his health insurance card. The woman typed a few things into the computer and printed out a bracelet that she placed on Sarah's wrist.

"You two can have a seat and someone will call you back when they are ready for you," she said.

Charlie led Sarah over to a bench where they sat down. He placed an arm around her back and rubbed the side of her arm. She laid her head on his shoulder and he kissed the top of her head. They sat like that for about 10 minutes before a door opened.

"Sarah Simmons?" a nurse asked.

Sarah had yet to legally change her last name to Canton.

"Here," Sarah said as she and Charlie stood up and walked toward the nurse.

The nurse led them inside a room where he closed the door.

"What are you here for today, Ms. Simmons?" the nurse asked.

"Actually, it's Mrs.," Charlie interrupted.

Sarah glanced at Charlie before turning her attention back to the nurse.

"I'm almost 13 weeks pregnant and I woke up to some blood near my vagina this morning," she said calmly.

"I see," he replied. "And have you had any other bleeding so far during your pregnancy?"

"No, this is the first time," she responded.

"Are you experiencing any pain or cramping?" he asked.

"No," she replied.

"Good. Let's take your vitals and we'll get you back in a room to get you looked at," the nurse said.

He took Sarah's blood pressure and her temperature. After inputting her information into a computer, he led her and Charlie to a hospital room. Sarah sat herself on the bed and Charlie stood next to her.

"I'm going to have you change into this gown and a doctor will be with you shortly," the nurse said before leaving the room.

Charlie helped Sarah out of her clothes and into the hospital gown. Then he began to pace back and forth across the floor. He didn't want to wait any longer. He wanted someone to tell them everything was OK, that the baby was fine, and this was normal. The baby had to be OK for Sarah's sake, he thought. She had been through so much this summer, she couldn't lose the baby too, he thought. He stopped pacing and looked over at his wife.

"I wasn't expecting to be back here so soon," she said, cracking a smile.

Charlie let out a light laugh and walked over to her side. He grabbed her hand and brought it to his lips, giving it a light kiss. He lowered her hand but kept holding it. He wanted to tell her everything was going to be OK, but he couldn't. He didn't know that.

Sarah examined her husband's face. She wondered what he was thinking about. She could tell he was nervous, but she didn't know what to say to calm his nerves because she was nervous too. She was scared. She didn't want Charlie to blame her if something had happened to the baby.

There was a knock at the door and then a doctor entered the room. Sarah and Charlie turned to look at her. Sarah was pleasantly surprised to see a female doctor. She heard horror stories of how women who experienced miscarriages were treated in emergency rooms and she hoped a female doctor would be more understanding – if that was indeed what she was going through, Sarah thought.

"Hi, Sarah. My name is Dr. Randolph. I understand you've experienced some bleeding this morning?" she asked as she approached the couple.

"Yes. I woke up to a small pile of blood this morning," Sarah responded.

"Have you experienced any other bleeding or spotting throughout your pregnancy?" Dr. Randolph asked.

"Not that I'm aware of," she answered.

"And you don't have any abdominal pain right now?" the doctor asked.

"No," Sarah responded.

"OK, good. I'm going to push on your stomach in a few places and you let me know if you experience any pain, OK?" the doctor said.

"OK," she said.

Dr. Randolph used two fingers to push down in a few spots around Sarah's stomach. Charlie watched Sarah's face for any signs of pain, but her face remained content.

"Did that hurt at all?" the doctor asked.

"No," Sarah responded.

"OK, well that's a good sign. I'm going to have someone come get you to take you back for an ultrasound so we can make sure the baby is OK," the doctor said.

"OK," Sarah said.

Dr. Randolph exited the room and Charlie let out a sigh of relief.

"That sounds good," he said.

Sarah smiled up at him. She wasn't convinced. She had to hear her baby's heartbeat to make sure everything was OK. She looked down at her stomach and rubbed it with her hand. Charlie placed his hand over hers and held it there. Then a nursing assistant walked into the room.

"Hi, Mr. and Mrs. Simmons," she said.

Charlie let out a light laugh. It was better than referring to Sarah as miss, he thought.

"My name is Hillary and I'm going to take you back to the ultrasound room. Are you ready?" she asked.

Sarah nodded her head. Hillary and Charlie helped Sarah off the bed and into a wheelchair. Charlie pushed the wheelchair as they followed Hillary to the room. He helped Sarah out of the chair and onto the bed. The ultrasound technician handed her a sheet to place over her legs. Afterward, she had Sarah hike the gown up to show her stomach.

The technician squeezed a clear gel over Sarah's stomach that caused her to shiver briefly. Charlie grabbed Sarah's hand as the technician moved the probe over the gel. The monitor was turned away from them so they couldn't see the imaging. The technician didn't say anything as she continued to move the probe.

Charlie's heart was beating so fast. This was the moment of truth. He hoped with all his heart everything was going to be OK, but he wasn't sure it was. And if it wasn't, he didn't know what he could do to console Sarah. He looked at his bride. Her eyes were closed. He gave her hand a light squeeze and she opened her eyes at him. He blew her a silent kiss and she smiled.

"OK," the technician said, breaking the silence.

Sarah and Charlie turned toward her.

"I'm not supposed to show you this, but I want to give you some relief," she said as she turned the monitor toward them.

She moved the computer mouse over a white blob on the screen.

"You see this white circle? That's your baby's head," she said.

Charlie squeezed Sarah's hand as she let out a sigh of relief.

"And this," the technician said moving the curser down the baby's body, "is your baby's heartbeat."

"Oh my God," Sarah exclaimed as she cried happy tears. "I didn't lose it?"

"Nope. There is very much a baby in there," the technician said.

Charlie leaned closer to the screen.

"That's our baby," he said, smiling at Sarah.

She nodded her head yes as tears continued to fall down her face. Charlie leaned down and hugged Sarah. She wrapped her arms around him tight.

"I love you," she whispered in his ear.

He kissed the top of her head.

"I love you too," he whispered back.

Sarah turned her attention back to the technician.

"So is the baby OK?" she asked.

"That, I'm not sure of. All I can tell you is the baby is there and has a heartbeat. I'm going to take some photos for the doctor to look at and she will be able to determine what happened from there," the technician responded.

"OK," Sarah said.

The technician moved the monitor back toward her and took photos as she continued moving the probe over Sarah's stomach. After a few moments, she removed the probe and wiped the gel off of Sarah's stomach.

"OK. We are all done here. You can head back to your room and the doctor should be in shortly," the technician said.

Sarah moved her gown back into place and swung her legs off the side of the bed. Charlie helped her into the wheelchair and wheeled her back to their room. Once in the room, he closed the door and helped Sarah onto the bed.

"We're still having a baby," he said excitedly.

"Yes, we are," she said, smiling at him.

Charlie leaned down and kissed her on the lips.

"You have no idea how relieved I am, Sare-bear. I am so excited to start a family with you," he said.

"Me too," she said.

She reached her hand out and grabbed Charlie's hand. She was relieved she hadn't lost the baby, but she was still wary something was wrong. She could tell Charlie's nerves had vanished and she wished hers had as well, but something still felt off to her. She tried to push those feelings aside and focus on the fact she was still carrying a baby.

There was a light knock at the door and then Dr. Randolph entered the room. She approached Charlie and Sarah and took a seat on the stool in the room.

"I have some good news. You did not lose the baby. It is still there and appears to be healthy," she said.

"That's great news," Charlie replied.

Sarah smiled at her husband, but she could sense there was more.

"However, the ultrasound showed some polyps on your cervix. That explains the mild bleeding you had this morning. Right now, the polyps are small and are not cause for concern, but you will want to follow up regularly with your doctor. If the polyps grow, that could increase your risk for a miscarriage," Dr. Randolph said.

Sarah was silent as she processed this information.

"But right now, it's nothing to worry about?" Charlie asked.

"I wouldn't say it's nothing to worry about, because you definitely want to keep an eye on it. But for now, it's nothing to lose sleep over," she replied.

"Thank you, doctor," Charlie said.

Dr. Randolph turned her attention back to Sarah.

"Do you have any questions, Sarah?" she asked.

"Is this common? Is there something I did to cause this? Is there anything I can do to make it go away?" Sarah asked.

"Polyps can be common. Some women get them and some don't. There really isn't any explanation for them. The only way for them to go away is to have them removed, but that is not recommended unless they become an issue," Dr. Randolph said.

"I see," Sarah said.

"I wouldn't worry about it too much. Just make sure you follow up with your doctor so he or she can keep an eye on it," she said.

"Will do. Thanks," Sarah said.

"Do either of you have any other questions?" Dr. Randolph asked.

Charlie looked at his wife. She shook her head no.

"I think we're all set, doc. Thanks," he said.

"OK. Well, I don't have anything else for you. So once you are dressed you are free to go," she said.

The doctor left the room. Charlie turned toward Sarah and performed a little happy dance. She let out a laugh. He walked toward her smiling ear to ear.

"Everything is OK," he said.

"Yeah," she said, returning the smile.

5

The morning after Sarah's miscarriage scare, Charlie woke up early to surprise her with breakfast in bed. He made pancakes with peanut butter and chocolate chips on top, just the way she liked them. He arranged the pancakes on a plate, which he placed on a tray with a glass of orange juice and a single rose that he clipped from one of the bushes outside the house. He carried the tray upstairs to her bedroom and placed it on the end table next to her bed. She was still sound asleep. Charlie leaned down and kissed her on the forehead. Sarah slowly opened her eyes and smiled up at him.

"Good morning, beautiful," he said.

"Good morning," she said, rolling onto her side to face him.

"I made you breakfast," he said, motioning toward the tray.

Sarah moved her eyes toward the tray.

"You didn't have to do that," she said, smiling at him.

"I know, but I wanted to," he replied.

Sarah sat up and leaned her back against the headboard. Charlie lifted the tray up and placed it on her lap. He moved to the other side of the bed and climbed in next to her. Sarah cut into the pancakes and took a bite.

"Mmm," she said as the melted peanut butter touched her tongue.

Charlie smiled at her.

"I am the luckiest girl in the world," she said, looking at him.

"Yes, you are," he said laughing.

Sarah smiled at him. She continued eating the pancakes until every bite was gone. She rested her hands on her stomach and let out a satisfactory sigh. She turned her head toward her husband.

"What would you like to do today?" she asked.

"Well, you have physical therapy today at 11," he replied.

"Fuck," Sarah said.

She had forgotten about her therapy. She was scheduled to go three days a week for the next three weeks and then they were going to reconvene from there. She had improved tremendously since waking up from her coma, but she still had a ways to go in her recovery. She suffered from fatigue and could only be awake for a few hours at a time. She also experienced spurts of brain fog that caused her to lose her train of thought.

Her doctors were convinced that would go away over time with the help of therapy. Sarah would be able to return to work once that happened. The owner of the bookstore Sarah worked at was very understanding and told Sarah she would be welcomed back when she was ready. But Sarah wasn't in any rush to return to work. She knew she had to take the time to fully recover. She was also enjoying the extra time with her husband.

"What are you going to do?" she asked.

"After I drop you off, I was going to head to my apartment to grab a few more things to move over," Charlie replied.

"Does this mean you're finally moving in?" Sarah asked playfully.

"Finally? I just brought you home two days ago," he said laughing.

"I know, but we've been married for two weeks! We should be living together by now," she said.

"We are. Don't worry. I'm not going anywhere," he said.

Charlie leaned over and kissed her lightly on the lips.

"I am here for the long run," he said.

"Good. Because we have a lot of making up to do," she said.

"Making up?" Charlie asked confused.

"Uh, yeah! We've been married for two weeks and we've only consummated our marriage once," Sarah said.

Charlie's eyes widened. He didn't think Sarah would want to have sex for a while after the miscarriage scare. He leaned down and kissed her hard on the mouth.

"I'll try to squeeze that into my busy schedule," he said, giving her a wink. "In the meantime, you should get ready. We need to leave soon to get you to your appointment."

Sarah grumbled.

"Let's just stay in bed all day," she said as she tried to pull Charlie toward her.

He let out a laugh.

"I wish we could, babe. Trust me. But this is important," he replied.

"So is this," she said with a playful grin.

Charlie laughed again.

"We have plenty of time for that later," he said as he climbed out of bed.

He walked toward Sarah's side of the bed. He leaned down and kissed her forehead.

"But for now, you need to get ready. We need to leave in 20 minutes," he said.

He lifted the tray off of her lap and walked toward her bedroom door.

"Fine," she grumbled.

He let out a light laugh as he carried the tray downstairs and into the kitchen. Meanwhile, Sarah climbed out of bed and got ready. She met Charlie downstairs about 15 minutes later. He drove her to her appointment and then went to his apartment. He checked the mail on his way up since it had been about a week since he was last there.

There was a letter from his health insurance company. He carried it, along with the rest of his mail, up to his apartment. Once inside, he immediately opened the letter. It stated his benefits were ending in two months since he was no longer an active military member. He knew his health insurance was only good for six months after leaving the military, but he had lost track of time. His plan was to find employment before that happened, but there wasn't much time left. He knew he couldn't let his insurance lapse with Sarah's medical needs.

He knew he had to find a job with benefits and fast. Aside from Sarah needing health insurance, his savings were dwindling. Sarah had some money saved from her inheritance when her dad died, but Charlie didn't want to rely on that. He wanted to be able to support his growing family.

He also didn't want to worry Sarah. So he decided not to tell her about the insurance issue. Instead, he hid the letter in a drawer in his apartment. He knew the news would only stress her out and she was already under enough stress with her recovery, he thought.

He had no idea what he wanted to do for work, but that didn't matter. He didn't have time to be picky. He powered up his laptop and began searching for job listings in the area. There was an immediate opening at a local construction company. The job didn't require any prior experience, which qualified Charlie for the position.

It wasn't his ideal job, but the pay was good - and it included health benefits. Charlie was used to manual labor and would be able to handle that aspect of the job. He decided to apply for the position. He submitted his resume and a cover letter online. Just as he hit submit, his phone began to ring. It was Sarah.

"Hey, babe," he said as he answered the phone.

"Where are you?" she asked.

Charlie looked at the clock on his laptop. It was 12:10 p.m. He was supposed to pick Sarah up at noon.

"I'll be there soon. I got stuck in traffic," he lied.

"Oh, OK. I'm outside waiting," she replied.

"See you soon," he said as he hung up the phone.

"Fuck," he said out loud.

He quickly powered his laptop off and rushed out the door. Stuck in traffic, he thought to himself. He had never lied to Sarah before. He could have just told her he was applying for a job, but he didn't want her to ask questions and find out about the issue with their health insurance. He also didn't want her to know he had applied for the job in case he didn't get it.

He sped the whole way to Sarah's therapy facility. He made it there in five minutes, when it would usually take 10. He pulled into the parking lot and Sarah was sitting on the curb outside. She got up and made her way to the car.

"I'm sorry I was late," Charlie said as she got inside.

"It's OK," she said.

"How was it?" he asked as he pulled out of the parking lot.

"It was painful," she replied.

"I'm sorry, babe," he said as he placed a hand on her leg.

"These next three weeks are going to suck," she said.

"Yeah, but it will be worth it. You'll be nice and strong again," Charlie said.

Sarah laughed. She had never considered herself strong. Charlie smiled at her.

"Do you want me to get you anything on the way home?" he asked.

"No, I'm pretty tired. I kind of just want to go home and nap," she said.

"OK, sounds good," he said.

A few minutes later, they arrived home. Charlie went to help Sarah out of the car.

"Do you need help carrying your stuff inside?" she asked.

"Stuff?" Charlie asked.

"You said you were going to your apartment to bring some more of your stuff over," Sarah replied.

"Oh, yeah," he said, realizing he forgot to pack anything. "It's still at my apartment. I'm going to have to go back."

Sarah eyed him suspiciously.

"I have more stuff than I anticipated," he said nervously.

"OK," she said as she walked toward the front door.

Charlie followed behind. He could sense she was becoming suspicious, but he didn't know what else to do. He hoped after her nap she would forget about it. He helped her inside the house and upstairs to her bedroom. She climbed into bed and Charlie kissed her on the forehead.

"I'm going to go back to my place to continue packing. If you need anything, just let me know," he said.

"I can come with you," she said.

"No, that's OK. You stay here and nap. I'll be back soon," he replied.

"OK," Sarah said.

Charlie left and drove back to his apartment. Sarah laid in bed awake. She could sense Charlie was lying to her, but she didn't understand why. He had never lied to her before, at least not that she knew of. She had always trusted Charlie and she didn't want to not trust him, especially now that they were married. She decided to push those thoughts out of her head and told herself there wasn't anything to worry about. After doing so, she quickly fell asleep.

Meanwhile, Charlie was at his apartment packing up his clothes. He felt guilty about lying to his wife, but that was the only option he could come up with. He knew stress wasn't good for the baby, and he didn't want to add to that. He also knew the main reason, and possibly the only reason, Sarah married him was for his health insurance.

If he could no longer give her that, he didn't know what that meant for their future. They had grown together since their wedding and he felt their relationship was stronger than ever. He didn't see that changing, even without health insurance. But the thought lingered in the back of his head. He decided not to focus on that and instead focus on resolving the problem. Once the problem was resolved, he would tell Sarah everything, he decided.

Charlie finished packing his clothes and looked around his apartment. All of his bathroom supplies were already at Sarah's house. The only thing that remained at his apartment was his furniture. He and Sarah never discussed what pieces, if any, they wanted to keep. So she would have to come back with him for that, he decided. He loaded his clothes and laptop into his car and drove back home.

Sarah was sound asleep when he arrived. Charlie wanted to unpack his clothes, but he and Sarah never discussed where they would go. There wasn't any room in her closet and Edward's room was exactly the way it was before he died. To Charlie's knowledge, Sarah still had not entered her dad's bedroom since his passing. It was a bigger room and had more closet space, but Charlie understood why Sarah wouldn't want to move in there.

For the meantime, he decided to hang his clothes in the closet in the guest bedroom. It was a small closet, but he could at least hang his dress clothes in there, he decided. He was almost done hanging up his shirts when Sarah walked in.

"What are you doing?" she asked.

"Oh, hey babe," Charlie said. "I was putting some of my clothes in here because I didn't know where else to put them."

"Oh," Sarah said.

She never thought about where Charlie's things would go once he moved in. The house was how it was when her dad died, and she didn't want to change that. Keeping things as they were helped her feel at home even though her dad was no longer there. She missed him more than she cared to admit.

"I hope that's OK," Charlie said, reading Sarah's face.

"Um, yeah. That's fine. We can find a place for the rest of your things," she said.

"OK, cool," he said.

He hung up his last few shirts and walked over to his bride. He wrapped his arms around her and pulled her into a hug. She hugged him back and pressed the side of her face against his chest. She could feel his heartbeat through his shirt. It made her feel a sense of peace. In that moment, she had forgotten about Charlie lying to her earlier in the day.

She lifted her head up and smiled at him. He returned the gesture. He leaned down and kissed her firmly on the lips. She playfully grabbed his upper lip with her teeth and gave him a wink. Charlie lifted her off the ground and she wrapped her legs around his waist.

He pinned her back against the wall and began kissing her neck. The feeling of his warm breath against her neck began to make her wet. She wanted Charlie and she didn't want to wait. She grabbed his shirt and lifted it over his head. She dropped it on the ground.

She grabbed his face with her hands and pulled it toward her face. She forced her tongue into his mouth. Their moment of passion was interrupted by the sound of the doorbell. Charlie pulled his head back and looked down the hallway.

"Ignore it," Sarah said.

He leaned back in and kissed her hard on the lips. Then the doorbell rang again. Charlie pulled away and placed Sarah's legs back on the ground.

"No," she whined.

"I'm just going to go see who it is. I'll be right back," he said.

He walked out into the hallway, but then turned back around. He eyed Sarah's body up and down. Then he bit his lower lip.

"My wife is sexy," he said.

Sarah smiled. Charlie turned away and walked down the steps to the front door. He opened it and was surprised to see his parents standing on the front steps. They were holding takeout containers. Then he remembered they made plans to come over for dinner.

"Did we come at a bad time?" his mom asked as she observed his bare chest.

Charlie followed her gaze and realized he wasn't wearing a shirt.

"Or a good time," his dad joked.

Charlie let out a laugh and nervously placed his arms across his chest.

"No, you're good. Sarah was just upstairs napping. Come on in," he said as he stepped aside to let them in.

"How is she doing?" Marie asked as they entered the house.

"She's doing pretty good. She started physical therapy today so she's a little sore. But other than that, she's pretty good," Charlie replied.

"I'm glad to hear that," Ray said.

"Yeah. Well, if you two want to take the food into the kitchen, I'll go wake her up," Charlie said.

"Actually, I'm already awake," Sarah said as she appeared at the top of the stairs.

"Well good morning, sunshine," Charlie said jokingly.

Sarah gave him a smile as she walked down the steps toward him.

"Hello, Mr. and Mrs. Canton," Sarah said.

"Please, call us mom and dad," Marie said.

Sarah politely smiled. She didn't mind calling Marie mom, but she would never be able to call Ray dad. She only had one dad and no one else could ever live up to that title, she thought.

"Well, shall we eat?" Ray asked.

"I'm going to go put a shirt on and I'll meet you guys in the kitchen," Charlie responded.

Charlie went upstairs and Sarah led his parents into the kitchen where they sat down at the table. Charlie entered the room a moment later. The Cantons brought Chinese takeout for dinner.

"My favorite," Sarah said as she placed some food onto her plate.

"A little birdy may have told us that," Ray said, giving her a wink.

Sarah smiled back at him.

"So how is the baby doing?" Marie asked.

Sarah looked up at Charlie. She wondered if he mentioned the polyps to his parents. He slightly shook his head no as if he were reading her thoughts. She liked that about Charlie. They knew each other so long they could communicate without words. She looked back at her mother-in-law.

"The baby is doing good," she said.

"That's wonderful. How far along are you now?" Marie asked.

"Almost 13 weeks," Sarah said excitedly.

"Wow. It won't be long now and you'll really start to pop," she said.

Sarah looked down at her stomach, which was already getting round.

"You'll still be beautiful," Charlie said.

Sarah looked up at him and flashed him a smile.

"Of course she will. She's a Canton now," Ray said, giving her another wink.

The four of them finished eating and then sat around the table making small talk for what felt like an eternity to Sarah. She wanted her in-laws to leave so she and Charlie could pick up where they left off. She let out a slight yawn. Ray looked down at his watch.

"I didn't realize it was getting so late. We should get going," he said to his wife.

"But we never get to see our son," Marie said.

"Mom, we live in the same town. We can see each other whenever we want," Charlie said.

"Fine. I can sense when I'm not wanted anymore," she said jokingly.

"Mom," Charlie said annoyed.

"I'm just kidding," she said.

Charlie rolled his eyes.

"Well, thanks for dinner. It was delicious," Sarah said.

"Thanks for having us over," Ray said.

"Any time," Charlie said as he stood up. "I'll walk you guys out."

Sarah stood up and gave her in-laws a hug before they disappeared into the living room with Charlie. She could hear them saying goodbye before she heard the door close. Charlie walked back into the kitchen.

"Shall we go back upstairs and finish what we started?" he asked with a grin on his face.

"Why go back upstairs?" she asked as she lifted herself onto the kitchen table.

6

The next day was the Saturday before fall officially began two days later. Charlie had made plans to surprise Sarah with a trip to the farmer's market. It was a tradition she and her dad did at the beginning of every season. This was going to be Sarah's first trip to the market without Edward. Charlie didn't know how she was going to take it, but he didn't want her to miss out on this tradition.

While she was still sleeping, he had picked out an outfit for her to wear and placed it on a chair next to her bed. He also included a note that read, *Put this on and meet me downstairs. I have a special day planned for us.* Downstairs, he had prepared a light breakfast for the two of them. He wanted to save room so they could grab something to eat at the market. He sat at the kitchen table and waited for his bride. She made her way downstairs about a half hour later.

"What are you up to?" she asked suspiciously as she entered the kitchen and saw the breakfast on the table.

"I can't do something nice for my wife?" he asked.

Sarah didn't respond. She just looked at him. She sat down at the table and began eating a bagel.

"So what are we doing today?" she asked.

"It's a surprise," Charlie responded.

Sarah rolled her eyes. She wasn't big on surprises. But if her husband wanted to do something nice for her, she wasn't going to stand in his way. After they finished eating, Charlie put everything away.

"Are you ready?" he asked.

"For what?" she replied slyly.

"You have to be patient, young grasshopper," Charlie said.

Sarah let out a laugh.

"Alright, let's go," she said.

The two of them got into the car and Charlie began driving them to the market. About five minutes into the drive, Sarah realized where they were going. She looked at her husband with tears in her eyes.

"Charlie," she said.

The last time she went to the market was the day before her dad died. It was their special tradition and they never missed it. She cherished those memories with her dad. But she wasn't sure she was ready to continue that tradition without him.

"I understand if you're not ready. I just thought it would be nice to go to honor Eddie's memory," Charlie said.

Sarah thought about that. If her dad were still alive, he would be going to the market today, she thought. That gave her a sense of peace. She wanted to be where he would have been, she decided.

"It's OK. I want to go," she said.

Charlie smiled at her and grabbed her hand. He pulled into the parking lot at the market a few minutes later. He put the car in park and the two of them stayed in the car. He looked at Sarah and knew she was thinking about Eddie. The last time they were at the market, they were with him.

But that was also the day he and Sarah took their relationship to the next level. Charlie couldn't help but think about that night. He could feel his penis grow slightly as he replayed the images of their lovemaking in his head. He quickly pushed those thoughts aside and focused on his wife.

"Are you ready?" he asked.

"Yeah, I think so," she said as she turned her head to look at him.

Charlie leaned over and gave her a light kiss on the lips. He got out of the car and walked over to the passenger side to help Sarah out. She grabbed his hand and the two of them made their way to the different booths.

"Where would you like to go first?" Charlie asked.

"We can just make our way around the different vendors," she replied.

The two of them began strolling down the aisles. Sarah stopped when she came across the painting booth she and her dad went to the last time they were there. He had bought a mountain painting that was now hanging in her living room. Her dad picked out that painting and one of a coastline. He asked Sarah which painting she liked better and she chose the mountain one.

She wondered if they still had the coastline painting. She entered the booth and began flipping through the paintings. She couldn't find the one her dad had previously picked out, but she found one that was similar. She pulled it out of the pile and held it up to Charlie.

"Do you like this one?" she asked.

"It's beautiful," he replied.

"OK. I'm going to get it," she said.

"I got it," Charlie said.

He grabbed the painting and went to the cashier to check out. While he did that, Sarah turned around and looked at the different booths. She pictured her dad at every single one of them. He loved going there. It was one of the few traditions they continued after her mom died.

Charlie approached her and grabbed her hand. She looked up at him and smiled. She was happy he took her there. Otherwise, she wouldn't have gone. Charlie knew how important that tradition was and she was happy he was there to uphold it.

"Where to now?" he asked.

"I'm hungry," she replied.

"Food trucks?" he asked.

"Food trucks," she responded with a smile.

They both decided on a chili dog and fries. It was what Edward ate the last time they were there. To Charlie, it made him feel like Edward was there with them. But he knew Sarah didn't believe in that sort of thing. To her, death was death and that was it. She looked up at him and smiled.

"Thanks for bringing me here today," she said.

"It won't be long and we'll have a little one coming here with us," he said, looking down at Sarah's stomach.

She smiled. She liked the idea of having a child to continue this tradition with. She looked down at her growing baby bump. As she did, she felt a sharp pain in her stomach. She grabbed her side and hunched over as she grabbed the picnic table for support.

"Are you OK?" Charlie asked concerned.

"I don't know," she replied.

"What can I do?" he asked.

"I'm going to go to the bathroom. I'll be right back," Sarah said.

She stood up and walked to the restroom. She entered one of the stalls and went to the bathroom. She looked down in the toilet and saw blood. There was more blood than there was a few days prior. She didn't know if it was another polyp or something more serious. She was concerned since she was experiencing pain this time. She didn't have any pain the other day.

She quickly wiped and washed her hands. She went back outside to find Charlie waiting by the restroom entrance for her. He looked at her and she could sense the fear in his eyes. She did everything she could to hold back her tears.

"Is everything OK?" he asked.

Sarah didn't know how to answer that question.

"We need to go to the hospital," she said.

"Are you bleeding again?" Charlie asked concerned.

Sarah nodded her head as she continued to hold back tears. Charlie grabbed her hand and they walked back to the car. He put the painting in the backseat as she climbed into the passenger side. He got into the driver's side and immediately started the car. He started driving to the hospital, neither of them saying a word.

They arrived to the hospital and checked in. They went through all of the same procedures as a few days prior. They found themselves sitting in the same hospital room with Sarah wearing a similar gown. They waited for a doctor to see them. Charlie was pacing back and forth across the floor as Sarah broke down into tears. He stopped pacing and looked at her.

Once he saw she was crying, he rushed to her side. He wrapped his arms around her and held her as she cried into his shoulder. He didn't know what to say. He didn't want to tell her everything was going to be OK, because he didn't know if it was. Instead, he just held her.

Their embrace was interrupted by a knock on the door. Charlie released his wife and she quickly wiped her tears away. He grabbed her hand, which was wet from the tears. He rubbed the droplets into her skin with his thumb. A doctor walked into the room. It was a different doctor than the one they saw the last time they were there.

"Hello, Mrs. Simmons. I'm Dr. Newman," he said as he approached Sarah and Charlie. "I see you're experiencing some bleeding again."

"Yeah," Sarah said. "There was more blood this time. I'm also experiencing some cramping in my lower abdomen."

Charlie looked at Dr. Newman's eyes. He was trying to read them for any sign of concern or relief. But they remained blank.

"OK. Well, we'll get you back into the ultrasound room to see what's going on," Dr. Newman said.

"OK, thank you," Sarah said.

Dr. Newman left the room. Charlie and Sarah waited for an assistant to come get them. Sarah was nervous to get the ultrasound. She knew something was wrong with the baby. She could feel it. She didn't know how she knew, but she could just sense it. She didn't want to share those thoughts with Charlie in case she was wrong. She hoped she was wrong. A few moments later, a woman walked into the room wearing blue scrubs.

"Sarah Simmons?" she asked.

"Yes," Sarah responded.

"OK. I'm going to wheel you back to the ultrasound room," the woman said.

"Can my husband come?" Sarah asked.

"Of course," the woman said.

The woman pushed Sarah in a wheelchair down the hallway as Charlie followed. They arrived to the ultrasound room a short while later.

"This is Sabrina. She is our ultrasound tech and she will assist you from here," the woman said before she walked away.

Charlie helped Sarah out of the wheelchair and into the bed.

"Hello," Sabrina said.

"Hi," Sarah replied.

Sabrina handed Sarah a sheet to cover herself with. After doing so, Sarah hiked up her gown to reveal her stomach. It already looked smaller to her, she thought. She knew her stomach wouldn't shrink that fast and it was all in her head, but she couldn't help but feel a sense of loss. She felt Charlie grab her hand. She looked over and gave him a slight smile. He didn't return the gesture. Instead, he blew her a kiss.

"Alright, let's take a look," Sabrina said as she squirted the cold gel onto Sarah's stomach.

She moved the probe across Sarah's stomach and hit buttons on her keyboard to take photos. She continued doing that in silence for a few moments.

"What can you see?" Sarah asked.

"I'm not at liberty to discuss that," Sabrina responded.

Charlie's stomach dropped. He knew that wasn't a good sign. He lightly squeezed Sarah's hand and she looked at him with panic in her eyes. He didn't know what to do to make her feel better.

"Can you at least tell us if the baby is OK?" he asked.

"It's not my job to interpret the photos. I just take them and then the doctor will analyze them for a final diagnosis," she said.

Sarah glared at the technician before quickly changing her facial expression. She did not like this woman. She was sitting there trying to hold it together while being afraid she lost her child, and this woman was not doing anything to ease her concerns.

"OK, well we are all set here," Sabrina said as she wiped off the gel from Sarah's stomach. "If you want to head back to your room, the doctor should be in shortly."

"Thanks," Charlie muttered.

He helped Sarah back into the wheelchair and pushed her back into their room. He closed the door and Sarah walked over to the bed. She lifted herself onto the side of the bed and began to cry. Charlie rushed to her side and held her. He didn't know what to do. He wanted to cry too, but he felt he needed to be strong for his wife. So he just held her in silence.

"I don't know why she couldn't tell us something to let us know what's going on," Sarah stuttered in-between sobs.

"I know, babe," Charlie responded.

He continued to hold her until there was a knock on the door. Dr. Newman walked into the room. Once again, Charlie couldn't read his face. He sat down on the stool and scooted closer to the bed.

"There's no easy way to say this, so I'm just going to come out and say it," he said. "You are having a miscarriage."

"What do you mean by having?" Charlie asked.

"I mean, Sarah has already passed some of the pregnancy tissue but there is still some inside her uterus," the doctor said.

Sarah started crying again. Charlie put his arm around her lower back and began rubbing it.

"What can we do?" Charlie asked.

"We are going to prescribe her some medicine that will allow her to pass the remaining tissue," Dr. Newman said.

"We can't reverse this?" Charlie asked.

"The pregnancy is no longer viable," the doctor replied.

"Was it something I did?" Sarah asked.

"That's not likely. Most miscarriages happen because the fetus is not developing normally. It could be an issue with the egg or something else that is out of your control," he said.

That gave Sarah a small sense of relief that it wasn't her fault. But she still felt guilty about losing her baby. She loved her baby more than she had ever loved anything and now it was gone. She felt a sense of loss she had never experienced before. She thought she was crazy for feeling this way about something she had never met. But she couldn't help it.

"Do you have any questions?" the doctor asked.

"Will this medicine make her sick? Will she experience any pain while…," Charlie paused.

It was hard for him to say the words.

"While passing the tissue?" Dr. Newman asked.

Charlie nodded his head.

"No. The feeling will be similar to going to the bathroom while on your period," he responded.

Sarah hated that he just compared losing her baby to having a period. They were not the same thing. One was shedding tissue from your uterus and the other was passing a dead baby, she thought to herself. She wanted to break down and cry again, but she held it together. She looked at Charlie and wondered what was running through his head.

"How long will it take?" Charlie asked.

"It should only take a few days. She will need to follow up with her OBGYN in a week to make sure all of the tissue has passed," Dr. Newman said.

Charlie looked at Sarah.

"Do you have any questions, babe?" he asked.

Sarah shook her head no. Charlie looked back at the doctor.

"OK. Well if there's nothing else, here's the slip for your prescription. And we are all set," the doctor said.

Charlie grabbed the piece of paper from Dr. Newman. The doctor gave Sarah a half-smile before leaving the room. As soon as the door closed, Sarah broke down crying. Charlie wrapped her up into a hug and held her. This time, he cried with her.

"I know, baby. I know," he said.

They held each other and cried for about five minutes. Charlie was heartbroken they weren't going to have a baby. He was looking forward to starting a family with Sarah. Even though the pregnancy wasn't planned, it brought the two of them back together. And Charlie would forever be grateful for that.

He was worried about what would happen between them now. There wasn't a baby tying them together anymore. And if Charlie lost his health insurance, which he was slated to do, there wouldn't be anything keeping Sarah from leaving him, he thought. He knew she loved him, but he couldn't help but think she might go back to Tim. After all, she did it before.

He knew he was being selfish thinking about that when his wife was grieving just as much, if not more, than he was over the loss of their baby. He decided to push those thoughts aside and focus on her. He didn't know what to do, but he knew he wanted to make her feel better. He was going to be there for her, and their relationship would come out stronger than ever, he decided.

"Let's get out of here," he said.

Sarah nodded her head. Charlie helped her out of the gown and back into her clothes. They left the hospital and drove to the pharmacy. Charlie dropped off the prescription and the pharmacist told him it would be about an hour wait.

"Do you want to go home or do something else while we wait?" he asked.

"Can we go to the cemetery?" Sarah asked.

The cemetery where Edward was buried was about a five-minute drive from the pharmacy. Sarah hadn't been there since before the crash. Charlie was surprised she wanted to go there now.

"Of course," he said.

He drove the two of them to the cemetery. Sarah was quiet the entire drive there. He parked the car near Edward's grave. Sarah got out of the car without saying anything. Charlie didn't know if he should follow or stay in the car. He decided to stay in the car. Then Sarah turned around and looked at him. So he got out of the car and went and stood next to his wife. She grabbed his hand.

He looked at her and realized he had never loved her more than he did in that moment. She had suffered extreme tragedies during the past few months, and she was still standing there stronger than ever. He was amazed at her strength. She never looked more beautiful to him.

"I love you so much," he said.

She gave him a wry smile.

"I love you too," she said.

She sat down on the grass next to the grave. The dirt from the burial was no longer visible. That was the only thing that had changed from the last time she was there.

"What's up, Eddie," Charlie said as he sat next to her.

Sarah let out a light laugh. She didn't believe in talking to tombstones. She didn't believe in spirits or an afterlife. To her, her dad was gone forever. But Charlie ignored her and continued talking to the stone.

"We really miss you down here," he said.

Sarah looked at her husband with admiration. She wasn't going to make fun of his beliefs. Especially if it helped him cope with the loss of her dad. She knew they were close with each other.

"A lot has happened since you've been gone," Charlie continued.

"Yeah. For starters, Charlie and I got married, dad," Sarah chimed in.

Charlie looked at her surprised. He knew her beliefs, or lack thereof. She shrugged her shoulders at him.

"It doesn't hurt. Worst case scenario, I'm talking to a stone. Best case scenario, I'm having a conversation with my dad," she said smiling.

She didn't believe the latter, but it was a nice thought. Charlie smiled at her. This girl continued to surprise him, he thought. The two of them took turns telling Edward everything that happened since he died, from the car crash to the miscarriage. The pain of the loss of their baby was too much for either of them. They cried while talking about it, but they held each other for support.

Sarah felt a light breeze brush against her. It gave her a sense of peace. She briefly thought about her dad but pushed that thought aside. It was nonsense, she decided. Or was it, she questioned herself. She closed her eyes and embraced the feeling. She pictured her dad hugging her. She opened her eyes and felt a sense of calm she hadn't felt since the last time she visited her dad's grave.

Charlie, completely oblivious to the possible spiritual awakening Sarah was experiencing, looked at his watch. It was time to pick up her prescription.

"Are you ready?" he asked.

She looked at him. She had a look in her eyes he had never seen before. He didn't know how to describe it, but she looked peaceful, he thought to himself.

"I am," she said.

They left the cemetery and picked up her prescription. They went home where they spent the rest of the evening in each other's arms.

7

About a week later, Sarah had her appointment with her gynecologist. She had been making big strides with her physical therapy and decided to drive herself to her appointment. This was the first time she drove since her car accident. It was a big step for her, and she was proud of herself for overcoming that fear.

She drove to her appointment where her doctor confirmed she had passed all of the remaining tissue. This meant she could stop taking the medicine she was prescribed. She felt a sense of relief. Every time she went to the bathroom and saw blood in the toilet, it was like losing her baby all over again. It took a big toll on her mental health and she was ready to move forward.

She decided to pick up Chinese food on the way home to surprise Charlie with dinner. She carried the takeout containers into the house and could hear him on the phone in the other room.

"Perfect. I will see you then," she heard him say.

She entered the kitchen where he was just getting off the phone.

"Who was that?" she asked.

"Oh, it was nobody," he replied.

Sarah looked at him quizzically.

"It was just my parents. I'm going to see them on Monday," Charlie said.

"Oh. What are we doing with them?" Sarah asked.

Charlie paused.

"Um, you'll be at physical therapy. I have to help my dad with something during your appointment," he lied.

He had received a call from the construction company he had applied at. He had an interview set up for Monday while Sarah was at her appointment. He didn't want her to know about the interview in case he ended up not getting the job. He also still didn't want her to know about the health insurance issue. She was under enough stress already with everything going on, he couldn't bear to add to that.

Sarah could sense he was lying to her again. It brought back all of the trust issues she felt a week prior. She replayed their conversation in her head from the week before. He said he was going to his apartment to pack up his things, but then showed up without anything, she thought. He was also late picking her up from her appointment, she added. Finally, he went back to his apartment and insisted on her staying home, she thought.

Now he was making secretive plans with his parents while she was away, she thought. Something didn't add up, she decided. She started to think Charlie was cheating on her. She didn't think he would ever do something like that, but the signs were there, she thought. She didn't want to press him on the issue because she knew he would continue to lie to her. Instead, she wanted him to think she believed him.

"Well, tell them I said hi," she said.

"I will," Charlie said smiling.

He hated lying to his wife. But at least this time she believed him, he thought. He was hoping to nail the interview and get the job. Once that happened, he would come clean to Sarah about all of his secrets, including their health insurance. He just had to get the job first, he thought.

"Thanks for dinner. I'm starving," he said as he dug into the food.

"No problem," Sarah replied.

She put a little bit of food on her plate, but she wasn't that hungry. She took a few bites out of an eggroll and placed it back on her plate. Charlie could sense something was wrong. It wasn't like her to pass up Chinese food.

"What's wrong, babe?" he asked.

Now was her chance. Should she confront him, she asked herself. She decided not to. That would only drive him further away, she decided.

"I'm just drained from everything," she said, which she decided wasn't a total lie.

She was drained. She had been through a lot in the past few months, more than most people have to endure in a lifetime. She lost her dad, almost died in a car crash, was in a coma for a month, and then lost her baby – all within the span of three months. She didn't know how she was handling all of that.

Then she looked over at Charlie and realized it was him. He was her rock. He was the one thing holding her together. But now, he was keeping things from her. And while she didn't want to suspect the worst, she couldn't help it.

"I get that. Is there anything I can do to help?" he asked.

She thought about that question. He had already done so much for her, she thought.

"Just continue being here for me," she said.

"Always," he responded.

She smiled at him. That was the answer she was hoping for. But that didn't ease her suspicions. The worst part of it all to her was that she didn't have anyone to talk to about her concerns. There was Tim, but they hadn't spoken since they broke up. She was certain he never wanted to see her again after that. But she made a mental note to reach out to him anyways.

"So how did it go at your appointment?" Charlie asked, interrupting her thoughts.

"Um, it went well. I passed all of the tissue, so that is done now. And the doctor said we could start trying to conceive again in a few weeks," she said.

"That's great news," Charlie said as his face lit up.

He was happy to hear they would be able to try again. He didn't know if Sarah wanted that, but he certainly did. Financially and mentally it may not be the best time, he decided. But he didn't care. He wanted to start a family with Sarah. He knew they would make great parents.

"Yeah," Sarah said, less enthusiastically.

"We don't have to," he said. "We can wait until you're ready."

"I know," she said.

"That doesn't mean we can't practice," he said, trying to lighten the mood.

Sarah laughed.

"I think we need lots of practice," she said smiling.

"Me too," Charlie said.

"We should practice tonight," she said, giving Charlie a wink.

"Really?" he asked.

They hadn't had sex in a week, and he wasn't expecting Sarah to want to so soon.

"Yeah," she said.

"I thought you said we had to wait a few weeks," he replied.

"That's to conceive. We can have sex whenever," Sarah said.

"Oh. I like the sound of that," he said.

"I'll meet you upstairs," she said as she got up from the table.

"OK," Charlie said grinning. "I'll clean up down here and I'll be right up."

"Don't take too long," she said, giving him another wink.

She went upstairs and slipped into her black lace bodysuit. She still had a slight bump on her belly, which the bodysuit enhanced. But she didn't care. She felt sexy in it. She hadn't worn it since her first time with Tim. The thought of that night and the feeling of Tim inside of her excited her. She tried to push the thoughts of Tim out of her head, but she couldn't. Tim was better in bed, she admitted to herself.

She laid on her bed in a seductive pose as she waited for her husband to come up the stairs. She continued to replay images of her and Tim in her head. She could feel herself getting wet. She felt guilty that he could still make her feel that way, but she couldn't help it. She wondered what her life would be like if she never got pregnant. She and Tim would probably still be together, and she never would have gotten into that accident, she decided.

She pushed those thoughts out of her head. It didn't change anything, she decided. She tried to focus on Charlie and the life they were building together. But images of her and Tim in the hot tub appeared in her head. She heard Charlie walking up the stairs. He walked into the room and his jaw dropped when he saw her.

"Damn," he said.

Sarah bit her lower lip at him. He quickly removed his shirt, revealing his muscles. Sarah's eyes dropped down his body. He moved his hands down to his pants and removed those as well. Sarah could see a slight outline of his penis through his underwear.

He made his way toward her. He crawled onto the bed, making his way on top of her. She started to pull the straps of her bodysuit down her arms.

"No, let me," he insisted.

Charlie pulled the straps down her arms and slowly pulled the rest of the bodysuit down her body until it was completely off. He sat back on his heels and admired her body. She felt self-conscious and covered her stomach with her hands. He pulled them away.

"You're beautiful," he said.

"No," she said as she pushed him on his back. "You're beautiful."

She climbed on top of him and kissed him hard on the mouth. She slid her tongue inside his mouth and danced it around his tongue. She retreated her tongue back into her mouth and began kissing her way down his body. She loved his muscles, she thought to herself as she made her way past them. She stopped when she got to his underwear.

Charlie lifted his hips off the bed as she removed his briefs. She tossed them to the floor. She made her way back to his manhood. It was partially erect, but not fully stiff. Sarah had a plan to change that.

She placed his penis in her mouth as she cradled his balls with her left hand. She moved her mouth up and down over his shaft as she swirled her tongue around it. Charlie let out a soft moan. Sarah pushed it further inside her mouth until the entire thing was covered. Charlie moaned again. She continued moving her mouth up and down over his phallus until he couldn't take it anymore.

Charlie forced her onto her back and thrusted himself inside of her. Sarah let out a painful moan. He quickly pulled his penis out of her vagina.

"Are you OK?" he asked concerned.

She nodded her head yes.

"Just go slow," she responded.

"OK. I'm sorry, baby," he said.

He slowly put the tip of his penis inside her. He left it there for a moment before pushing deeper. He moved in and out slowly until his penis was surrounded by her wetness. Then he began to thrust harder and faster. Sarah dug her fingernails into his back.

"Yes," she called out.

Charlie sat up while remaining inside of her. He grabbed her hips for support as he continued to pound into her. She moaned loudly. He began to grunt as he neared completion.

"No, don't stop," Sarah begged.

Charlie tried to make a grocery shopping list in his head to keep himself from ejaculating. He pictured himself going down the different aisles in the store. It was working. He could sense the feeling going away. He continued to thrust into his wife.

"Harder," she cried out.

He pushed into her as hard as he could. She let out a moan. He partially pulled himself out and did it again. She moaned louder. He continued pushing into her as hard as he could until he couldn't hold back anymore. He quickly pulled his penis out and covered the tip with his hand. He managed to catch most of his sperm with only a little bit dripping onto Sarah.

He ran to the restroom and cleaned up. He returned a few minutes later with a wet washcloth. He used that to wipe the residue off of Sarah. He put the washcloth in the laundry hamper in the bedroom. Then he climbed into bed naked with Sarah.

"Did you finish?" he asked.

"No, but that's OK," she said as she turned to face him.

"Well, let's change that," he said as he made his way toward her.

He gently grabbed her bottom lip with his teeth and gave it a playful pull. He kissed his way down her body until he reached her vagina. He circled his tongue around the outside of it before he thrusted it inside. She didn't taste as sweet as she normally did, but he didn't mind. He kept his tongue inside her. He flicked it up and down a few times before pulling it halfway out. Then he thrusted it back in as hard as he could.

"Just like that, baby," Sarah said.

Charlie did that a few more times before leaving his tongue inside her. He moved it back and forth as fast as he could. Sarah moaned so loud. He continued moving his tongue as fast as he could. It was growing tired and he thought it might fall off, but he pushed through. Then Sarah's legs began to tremble, and he tasted a release in his mouth.

He slowly pulled his tongue out and sat up. She was lying there in disbelief. She couldn't speak. Charlie was getting better at making her orgasm. He laid down next to her and smiled.

"How was that?" he asked.

Sarah couldn't respond. Her face was numb, and she was out of breath. Instead, she turned her head toward him and slowly gave him a thumbs up. Charlie laughed.

"I'm glad you enjoyed it," he said as he placed his hands behind his head.

He was quite pleased with himself. He was happy with her response. He rolled to his side and laid his head on her chest. He draped one of his arms across her stomach. Sarah placed her arm over his.

"Wow," she finally managed to say.

Charlie laughed again.

"That good, huh?" he asked.

Sarah turned her face to him.

"That was incredible," she said. "Can you do that every night?"

"I would love to make you feel like that every night. But honestly, I felt like my tongue was going to fall off," he said.

Sarah giggled.

"But I'll see what I can do," he said.

"You're the best," she said.

"Back atcha," he said.

He kissed her lightly on the lips and laid his head back down on her chest.

"I'm going to go to the bathroom really quick," she said as she picked his head up.

She got out of bed and left the bedroom. When she returned a few minutes later, Charlie was fast asleep. She crawled into bed next to him and cuddled up against him. While she had enjoyed the events that had just taken place, she couldn't help but be suspicious. He had never moved his tongue like that before with her. He must have learned it from someone else, she thought.

All of the evidence she had gathered convinced her Charlie was sleeping with another woman. While she didn't want to believe it, it was the only thing that made sense to her. She wanted to get more evidence, something substantial, before she confronted him about it, she decided. In the meantime, she was perfectly content letting him test out his new tricks on her, she thought. She fell asleep dreaming about their lovemaking. Then Charlie turned into Tim in her dreams.

8

Sarah woke up thirsty for Tim. She missed the way he touched her, the way he made her feel. She missed their dates and his knowledge of wine. She rolled over and saw Charlie staring at her. He wasn't a wine drinker. He was strictly a beer man.

"Good morning, beautiful," he said.

"Good morning," she replied.

He used his fingers to place a strand of hair behind her ear. It was a simple touch, but it made her forget about her thirst for Tim. She smiled at her husband. He leaned in and planted a kiss on her forehead.

"What do you want to do today?" she asked.

"I have some errands I have to run. But after that, I'm free," Charlie answered.

"What errands?" she asked curiously.

"I just have to pick up some things," he responded coyly.

"I can come with you," Sarah offered.

"No, that's OK. It's nothing fun. You just stay home and rest. When I get back, we can do something fun," he replied.

"OK," she said.

"Well, I'm going to go get ready," he said as he climbed out of bed.

He left the bedroom and went into the bathroom. Sarah heard the shower turn on a few minutes later. He was acting suspicious again, she thought. She wasn't ready to confront him just yet. She wanted to get a second opinion, a man's opinion. She grabbed her phone off of the end table and texted Tim. It was Saturday so she knew he wasn't working.

Hey! Can we meet up to talk today?, the text read.

She stared at her phone waiting for an immediate response, but it didn't come. She waited a few more minutes, but nothing happened. She placed her phone back on the end table. She got out of bed and walked toward her closet. She picked out a casual outfit to wear, which included jeans and a light sweater. September was nearing an end and the temperatures were beginning to drop in Indiana.

She placed the clothes on the chair in her bedroom and waited for Charlie to finish up in the bathroom so she could get ready. She went and checked her phone again. He still hadn't responded. She sat on her bed in frustration. He probably wasn't going to respond after what she did to him, she thought. She couldn't believe this was her first time reaching out to him after the breakup.

He deserved better, she thought. Then she heard the shower turn off. A few moments later, Charlie entered the bedroom wearing nothing but a towel wrapped around his waist. Water droplets were dripping down his abs. Sarah caught herself staring with her mouth partially open.

"What?" he asked confused.

Sarah closed her mouth and looked up at his face.

"I'm sorry, what?" she asked.

"You were looking at me weird," he said as he removed the towel and began to dry his hair with it.

"I was distracted by your beauty," she said.

Charlie let out a laugh.

"I don't think you realize how sexy you are," Sarah said.

"Oh really?" he asked as he approached her completely naked.

"Mhm," she nodded with excitement.

Then her phone let out a ping. She quickly grabbed it off of her end table. It was a response from Tim.

"Who is that?" Charlie asked.

"It's Aunt Susan. She's just checking in," she said nonchalantly.

Sarah was better at lying than Charlie, but she didn't like doing it.

"Oh. Well, tell her I said hi," he said as he turned back around.

He walked out of the bedroom. She quickly opened the text from Tim.

Hello! It's nice to hear from you. I can meet up today. What did you have in mind?, the text read.

Can I come to your house?, she responded.

Sure. How about six?, Tim texted back.

Sarah didn't want him to think it was a booty call. She also wanted to be home before Charlie got back so he wouldn't be suspicious. She looked at the time. It was 10:30 a.m.

Could we do noon?, she replied.
Noon works, he replied.
I'll see you then, she texted back.
See you, he responded.

Sarah grabbed her phone and went to find Charlie. He was in the spare bedroom getting dressed.

"I'm going to hop in the shower," she said.

"OK. I'll probably be gone by the time you get out, but I'll be back around 2. So think about what you want to do," he said.

"OK," she said.

She went to turn around, but Charlie grabbed her hand. He pulled her close and gave her a light kiss on the lips. She pulled away and he smiled at her.

"I love you, Sare-bear," he said.

"I love you too," she responded.

She walked into the bathroom and placed her phone on the counter. She closed the door and locked it. She didn't want Charlie to see she had been texting Tim. Even though the conversation was completely innocent, she didn't want him to become suspicious. She climbed into the shower and washed up.

Charlie was already gone when she got out of the bathroom. Sarah put on the outfit she had picked out and styled her hair. She applied a light coat of makeup on her face. She knew she wasn't going on a date, but she still wanted to look decent.

By the time she was done getting ready, it was time for her to head to Tim's house. Her heart was racing the whole drive there. She didn't know what she was going to say to him. She felt awful about the way things ended between them. She felt even more awful that she was going there to ask for advice on her marriage, but that didn't stop her.

She pulled into his driveway and she couldn't even think. Her heart was pounding so hard it drowned out her thoughts. She closed her eyes and did a quick breathing exercise to calm her nerves. Ten breaths later, she was ready to go inside. She exited her car and walked up his driveway toward his front door. She was about to knock on the door when it opened. Tim was standing there with a smile on his face.

"I heard you pull in the driveway," he said nervously.

Sarah wondered if he saw her sitting in her car as she hesitated to get out. She quickly pushed that thought aside and focused on the present.

"Hi," she said, giving him a shy wave.

"Come on in," Tim said as he stepped to the side.

Sarah entered the house and stood in the entranceway awkwardly. Even though she had been there several times before, it felt different to her this time. She didn't feel welcomed there.

"Can I get you something to drink?" Tim asked.

"Sure," she replied.

"What would you like?" he asked.

"I'll have whatever you're having," she said.

"Well, I'm going to have a glass of wine," he said as he looked toward her belly.

Sarah followed his gaze. He didn't know, she realized. She reflexively covered her stomach with her arms.

"I'm fine with wine," she responded.

"Oh?" he asked.

"I lost it," she said looking away.

"Oh, Sarah," he said as he walked toward her.

He grabbed her hands.

"I'm sorry," he said.

"Thanks," she said, looking up at him.

"So, wine it is," he said, changing the subject.

Sarah smiled. She hadn't had wine since the last time she was with him. She followed him into the kitchen as he pulled out two glasses. He grabbed a bottle of Pinot Grigio and poured it into the glasses. He placed the bottle on the counter and handed one of the glasses to Sarah.

"Cheers," he said as he clinked his glass to hers.

"Cheers," she said with a smile.

They both took a drink. Sarah licked her lips afterward. She noticed Tim was watching her. She quickly pulled her tongue back into her mouth and shyly smiled at him.

"So, how have you been?" he asked sincerely.

"I've been OK. I have a lot of appointments and physical therapy, which sucks. But it's been helping," Sarah replied.

"Good. I'm glad to hear that," he said.

She smiled at him.

"How have you been?" she asked.

"Well, it's been what, about four weeks now?" he asked.

That was it, Sarah thought to herself. During that time, she had gotten married, was released from the hospital, and lost her baby. It felt like so much longer than four weeks, she thought.

"So, I'm doing better. The first week was hard, really hard for me. But each week has gotten a little easier," Tim said.

Sarah gave him a half-smile. She didn't know how to respond to that.

"Not to sound rude or anything, but why are you here? Don't get me wrong, I was happy when you texted me. I'm just a little confused," he said.

"I know," she said. "Um, now that I'm here, I feel really stupid."

"What is it?" he asked.

"Well, there's some things going on with Charlie that I wanted to talk to someone about, but I don't really have anyone. And I've been thinking about you lately. So, I thought, maybe I could get your advice?" Sarah replied.

Tim placed his glass back down on the counter.

"I see," he said.

He had been hoping Sarah texted him because things were over between her and Charlie. He couldn't stop thinking about her. He began to text her 100 times over the last four weeks, but he could never bring himself to hit send. When he opened that message from her, his heart fluttered. He retyped his response half a dozen times before he actually replied. Now that she was there at his house, he felt dumb for letting himself think she wanted to get back together.

"I understand if that's weird or uncomfortable. I can just go," she said.

"No, you're already here. Let's go sit in the backroom and you can tell me what's going on," he said as he took her hand and led her to his three seasons room.

"I've always liked this room," she said, as she took a seat on the couch.

"A lot of fun was had in here," he said, giving Sarah a wink.

She blushed and took another drink of her wine. Tim took a seat on the opposite side of the couch.

"So what's going on?" he asked.

"Well, Charlie has been acting really suspicious lately and lying to me," Sarah said.

"How do you know he's lying?" Tim asked.

"I've known him almost my whole life. I can tell when he's not telling the truth," she responded.

"Right," Tim said.

He had forgotten Sarah and Charlie were lifelong friends. To him, Charlie was just the guy who stole his girlfriend now.

"I kind of feel like he's seeing someone else," she said.

Tim, who was about to take a drink, put his glass down and turned toward Sarah.

"As much as I hate to say this, Charlie loves you. That guy is head over heels in love with you. I don't think he would cheat on you," he said.

"That's what I thought too. But the evidence is piling up," she said.

"OK. What evidence?" Tim asked.

"Well, first, he drove me to one of my appointments and told me he was going to his apartment to pack up some of his things to move over. Then he didn't pick me up. I had to call him, and he told me he was stuck in traffic," she said as she made an annoyed face.

"Traffic in Muncie?" Tim asked jokingly.

"Exactly," Sarah said.

"OK. What else?" he asked.

"When he finally did show up, he didn't have any of his stuff. Then he dropped me off at home and told me he had to go back for it. I offered to go with him, but he insisted on going alone," she replied.

"Did he come back with his stuff?" Tim asked.

"Yeah," she answered.

"OK, so maybe he wasn't lying," he said.

"He was lying," she said.

"Is that all?" Tim asked.

"No, there's more. Then, I overheard him on the phone yesterday making plans to meet up with someone on Monday. He told me it was his parents, but when I asked what we were doing, he said it was during my physical therapy appointment," she said.

"Well, maybe that's true. That's not a far-fetched idea," he said.

"He was lying to me," Sarah said annoyed.

"Right," Tim said as he rolled his eyes.

"You know what, I'm just going to go. This was a mistake," she said as she stood up from the couch.

"No, please stay. I'm only messing with you," Tim said.

"Fine," she said as she sat back down.

"What else?" he asked.

"Today, he said he had errands to run. So I asked him where we were going, and he insisted on going alone. I told him I didn't mind, but he made it abundantly clear I was not invited," she said. "And I don't have any appointments or anything for him to use as an excuse."

"OK. Yeah, something about all of that is not adding up," he said.

"See? I'm not crazy," she said.

"Oh, you're definitely crazy," Tim said laughing.

Sarah leaned toward him and gave him a playful push. He laughed harder.

"I just don't think he would cheat on you," he said.

"I didn't either, but I don't know what else to think. So I wanted to get someone else's opinion," she said.

"I honestly think the best thing to do would be to confront him and find out why he's being so secretive," Tim said.

"If I do that, he's only going to keep lying," she said.

"That could be true. But you never know until you try," he said.

"I guess," she said.

"But hey, if he is cheating, and you want to get back at him, I'm always down," he said, giving Sarah a wink.

She laughed.

"I'll keep that in mind," she said while smiling at him.

She felt a rush. The thought of being with Tim again excited her. As she sat so close to him on the couch, she could feel the tension between them. Her thirst for him had returned. She wanted him.

He wanted her too. He could feel the sexual tension increase. He felt his penis grow as he pictured her naked body climbing on top of him. He bit his lower lip at her. His body was heating up.

Her heart was racing. She knew what she wanted, but she didn't want to hurt her husband. But he could be doing the same thing with someone else right now, she thought to herself. If that's the case, what's the harm, she questioned.

"Well, hopefully I was able to help a little bit," Tim said as he stood up.

"Oh," she said.

That caught her off guard. Did she just misread everything between them, she asked herself. She stood up and Tim led her to the front door.

"If you need anything, let me know. I'm still here for you, Sarah," he said.

"I appreciate that. And thanks for listening to me today," she said.

"No problem," he said as he leaned in and gave her a hug before quickly pulling away.

"Thanks again," she said as she walked out the door.

She got into her car and started driving home. What just happened, she asked herself. She replayed their conversation in her head. She thought they were flirting and there was some serious body language going on, she thought. But then he just kicked her out out of nowhere, she thought.

Meanwhile, Charlie was shopping for some new dress clothes for his interview on Monday. He didn't want Sarah to know about it because she didn't know about the interview. He already decided he was going to tell her he was with his dad picking up supplies for their project on Monday. He felt bad lying to his wife, but he thought he was doing so with the best intentions.

He picked out a new white dress shirt with a pair of navy dress pants. He also bought a new pair of brown dress shoes. He stored his new clothes at his apartment so he wouldn't raise suspicion from Sarah. He drove home and walked in to Sarah sitting on the couch, watching TV.

"How were your errands?" she asked.

"Good. We got all of the supplies we need for Monday," he replied.

"Oh. You were with your dad?" she asked.

"Yeah. He says hi, by the way," Charlie replied.

She wondered if she should call him out on his lies like Tim suggested. She decided not to.

"Do you want to go see a movie tonight?" she asked.

"Whatever you want," he replied.

9

Sarah woke up before Charlie on Monday morning. She snuck downstairs to the kitchen where she called her physical therapy office and asked if she could move her appointment back an hour. They allowed her to. She went back upstairs and climbed into bed.

"What were you doing?" Charlie asked as he pulled her close to him.

"I was just getting a drink," she lied.

Lying had become a habit between the two of them. But Charlie couldn't tell when Sarah was lying. He didn't think she had any reason to lie to him. Sarah on the other hand, had become very suspicious of him. She planned on trailing him to see where he was going.

The two of them laid in bed in silence as she mapped out her plan in her head. She was going to leave home at the time she normally would to head to physical therapy, but instead, she was going to park down the street and wait for Charlie to leave. She was playing out the different scenarios in her head when he interrupted her thoughts.

"You need to get ready for therapy, babe. It's almost time for you to leave," he said.

"Oh, shoot," she said as she looked at the clock.

It was 10:30 a.m. She usually left her house at 10:45 to make it to her 11 a.m. appointment. She jumped out of bed and quickly changed into workout clothes. She brushed her teeth, put on deodorant, and threw her hair in a ponytail.

"I'll see you later," she said.

"I might still be gone when you get home, but I shouldn't be too long," he said.

"OK," she said.

She walked downstairs and out the front door to her car. She drove down the street and parked a few houses down. She was far enough away where Charlie wouldn't recognize her car, but close enough where she could see him leave. About 15 minutes later, he walked outside and got into his car. He was wearing basketball shorts and a T-shirt.

Maybe he is helping his dad around the house after all, she thought to herself. He pulled out of the driveway and headed down the street in the opposite direction of Sarah. She turned her car back on and followed him from a distance. About 10 minutes later, he pulled into his apartment complex. He had moved everything to her house except his furniture, so she didn't know why he would be going there.

She parked in the back of the parking lot and watched him go inside his apartment. Her heart began to race as she prepared herself to see a woman enter his apartment. But there wasn't anyone else in the parking lot. About 15 minutes went by before Charlie left his apartment. He was wearing the new dress clothes he purchased a few days prior.

Sarah immediately thought he was dressed for a date. The thought of him having a job interview never crossed her mind. She was convinced her husband was cheating on her and seeing him all dressed up was the proof she was looking for. When she was planning her spy mission earlier in the day, she thought she would cry when she got the evidence she was looking for. But she didn't. She felt a sense of relief.

Seeing Tim the other day made her realize she still had strong feelings for him. She felt the energy between them and knew he felt the same. She loved Charlie, but there wasn't a baby tying them together anymore. She sat in her car and let different scenarios play out in her head. She thought about running to Tim immediately, but he was at work.

Despite everything she thought Charlie was doing behind her back, he was still her best friend. She didn't want to cheat on him, even though she thought he was doing the same to her. She was confused. She knew what she wanted, but she didn't want to hurt Charlie. She was also confused by her reaction to the thought of him cheating on her.

She had known Charlie most of her life and never thought he was capable of doing that to anyone, especially her. She knew he cared deeply for her, more than she could reciprocate. The thought of him cheating on her didn't make sense, but she didn't need it to make sense. She wanted to believe it because it gave her an out.

She knew she had been absent from the relationship lately. Losing the baby was hard on her and she mourned that loss internally. She kept most of her grief a secret from Charlie because she didn't think he would understand. She also had put him through a lot recently and she didn't want to add to that. So she fought that battle alone. She used that absence as a justification for him cheating on her.

She understood why he would want to be with someone else, someone who had less baggage. She had been through a lot that year and it damaged her, both physically and mentally. Who would want to be with someone who's broken, she thought to herself. She knew she jumped into marrying Charlie early, but she didn't have a choice.

She needed health insurance for her and her baby. But now that she was no longer carrying a baby and she was recovering well, it wasn't as urgent of a need. She could go without it until she was able to come up with a different solution, she thought. Her thoughts were interrupted by the sound of her phone ringing. She looked at the screen.

It was her physical therapy office calling. She looked at the time and realized she was late. She was supposed to be there 10 minutes ago. She had been sitting in her car processing her life for 45 minutes. She didn't answer the call. Instead, she let it go to voicemail.

There was no point in showing up this late, she decided. Her appointments were only an hour long and by the time she got there it would be halfway over. She turned her car back on and began driving home. She knew Charlie wasn't going to be there, but she didn't want to stay there. She wasn't ready to face him yet.

She needed more time to think. She needed a plan. She pulled into her driveway and got out of the car. She walked up the front steps and stared at the door for a moment before entering. The house still felt weird to her without her dad there. It was a feeling she was getting accustomed to, but she still didn't like it.

She didn't know where she was going to go, but she knew she wanted to get away from there. She went upstairs and packed a bag. It consisted of her toiletries and enough clothes to last her a few days. Sarah didn't know how long she was going to be gone, but she wanted to be prepared. She left the house with her bag. She was in a hurry and didn't leave a note behind.

She got into her car and began driving. She had nowhere to go and no plan. But she figured she would drive until she got tired and then find a place to spend the night. She had enough money on her to cover her meals and a hotel for a few nights.

About 10 minutes into her drive, Charlie called. She didn't answer. She let it go to voicemail. Her phone beeped, alerting her he had left a message. She didn't listen to it. She continued driving until she reached I-69. She decided to drive north toward Fort Wayne.

Her thoughts were racing faster than her car on the highway. There was too much to process and she couldn't concentrate on the road. She turned the music up in an attempt to drown out her thoughts. She tried to sing along to the radio to occupy her mind, but then a Mariah Carey song came on. She immediately thought about Charlie.

She should have left him a note, she realized. She knew he was going to be worried about her. She decided she would text him when she stopped to get gas. Then her phone began to ring again. It was Charlie. Nearly an hour had passed since his last call.

Once again, she didn't answer. Sarah was still getting use to driving again and she wasn't comfortable talking on the phone while doing so. Her phone beeped letting her know she had received another voicemail. She was nearing the Fort Wayne exit and decided to stop there to fill up her tank. Before getting out of her car, she decided to listen to Charlie's messages.

"Hey, babe. It's me. I just received a call from the receptionist at your physical therapy office saying you didn't show up for your appointment today. She sounded concerned since I guess you called to move your appointment back to noon today. So I was just calling to see what was going on. Call me when you get this. I love you," Charlie said in the first message.

She deleted that message and played the second one.

"Hey, babe. It's me, again. I'm starting to get concerned because I still haven't heard from you and you're not at home. Whatever is going on, please call me and we can talk about it. Whatever you're going through, we can get through it together. Just please, call me," he said in the second message.

She deleted that message as well. She sat in her car and stared at her phone in silence. She felt guilty. Charlie sounded really concerned for her, she thought. He didn't sound like someone who had just gone on a date with someone else, she decided. That made her feel even more guilty for thinking about running to Tim.

Sarah knew she should text Charlie and let him know she was OK, but she didn't know what to say to him. She didn't think he was cheating on her anymore. But that didn't change the way she felt. She had hoped he was cheating on her so she could be with Tim. She knew she needed to process those thoughts before talking to her husband.

She put her phone away and got out of the car. She filled up her tank and bought a few snacks at the gas station. Then she was back on the highway. She continued heading north, with no destination in mind. It was about an hour and a half since she left the gas station when her phone rang again.

This time, it was Tim. It was shortly after 3 p.m. and he would just be getting out of work, she thought. Her heart raced as she realized he had been thinking about her too. It wasn't like him to call her though. What if she had been with Charlie, she wondered.

"Hello?" she answered the phone.

She immediately wondered why she answered the phone like that, when she already knew who was calling.

"Sarah? Are you OK?" Tim asked concerned.

"Yeah, I'm fine. What's up?" she replied with confusion.

"Charlie called me," Tim started to say.

Sarah's heart sank. Tim wasn't calling her because he had been thinking about her. He was calling her because Charlie called him looking for her. She wondered if Charlie knew she went to Tim's house on Saturday. Her body began to fill with even more guilt.

"He's very worried about you. He said you didn't show up to your appointment this morning and you're not answering your phone. Is everything OK?" Tim asked.

"Um, I don't really know," Sarah answered.

"Well, what's going on? You can talk to me," he replied.

"You know how I thought he was cheating on me?" she asked.

"Yeah," he responded.

"Well, I kind of followed him and watched him get dressed up for what I thought was a date," she said.

"Oh shit. Really?" Tim asked.

"Yeah, but now I don't think it was a date. I don't know what it was, but I don't think he's cheating on me," Sarah said.

"I don't think so either," he replied.

"But, when I thought he was, I felt a sense of relief. I wasn't sad or hurt. I felt relieved. Because that gave me a reason to be with you. And I know that's selfish of me because I don't even know if you would want to be with me after what I did to you, but that's how I felt. And I wasn't ready to have that conversation with Charlie, so I left. And now I'm driving, and I've been driving for nearly three hours now," she said.

"Where are you?" Tim asked concerned.

"It looks like I'm about 20 miles away from Kalamazoo," Sarah replied.

"You're in Michigan?" he asked.

"I guess so," she said.

"Stop in Kalamazoo and I'll meet you there. I'll be there as fast as I can," Tim said.

"Please don't tell Charlie," she said.

"I won't. But I will tell him you're OK because he is worried sick about you," he replied.

"Thanks Tim," Sarah said.

"No problem. See you soon," he said before hanging up the phone.

Sarah put her phone down and continued driving to Kalamazoo. She didn't know what to do for three hours while she waited for Tim to get there, so she decided she would get a hotel room. Regardless of what Tim was going to say when he got there, she wasn't driving back to Muncie that night, she decided. She found a reasonably priced hotel downtown that was near a brewery.

She checked into the hotel and went upstairs to her room to take a nap while she waited for her ex-lover to arrive. Once she laid down on the bed, she couldn't fall asleep. Her heart was racing as she thought about being alone in the hotel room with Tim. Then she remembered his family lived in Kalamazoo and he would probably stay with them. But if he didn't, she wondered if anything would happen between them.

She didn't want to cheat on Charlie. And she didn't see Tim making a move while she was still married. He wasn't that type of guy, she thought. Then she thought about her husband. Her kind, gentle husband. He didn't deserve to be treated this way, she thought. She pulled out her cell phone and texted Charlie.

I'm OK. I have a lot of things I need to think about, and I needed to get away for a few days. That's all I really have to say right now. We will talk more when I get home. I'm sorry for making you worry, but I'm OK, the text read.

It was only a few seconds before he replied.

I'm glad you're OK. Take the time you need, and I'll be here when you get back. I love you, Sare-bear, he replied.

Sarah knew she didn't deserve Charlie. Their relationship was very one-sided with him putting in more than she returned. In theory, he was the perfect husband, she thought. But she couldn't shake her feelings for Tim. She fell asleep as she thought about the two men in her life.

10

The sound of Sarah's phone ringing woke her up. She rolled over in bed and looked at the screen. It was Tim calling.

"Hey," she answered sleepily.

"Hey! I'm just getting into town. Where are you?" he asked.

"I'm at the Green Inn," she answered.

"Are you in the lobby?" he asked.

"No, I got a room. It's 232," she said.

Tim was silent for a few moments.

"I'll be up in a few minutes," he finally said.

"OK," she said.

Sarah ended the call. Her heart was beating so fast. She was excited and nervous to be alone in the room with Tim. She remembered the energy between them just a few days prior. She wondered if that energy was going to feel stronger now that she admitted she wanted to be with him. What if he didn't want to be with her, she questioned.

She sat up on the bed and quickly brushed her hair with her fingers. The palms of her hands began to sweat as her nerves took over. She wiped them on the comforter and tried to focus on her breathing. It helped reduce the speed of her heartrate, but she was still nervous. Then there was a knock on the door.

She got off of the bed and slowly walked to the door. She opened it and Tim was standing there with a stern look on his face. He didn't look happy, she thought. He did just work a full shift and then drive three hours here on a work night, she added.

"Come in," she said as she stepped to the side.

He entered the room empty-handed. He didn't bring luggage so he must not plan on staying, Sarah thought. She felt silly for thinking he might. He sat down on a chair near the window.

"What are you doing, Sarah?" he asked almost exasperated.

"Well, I just took a nap," she responded.

"That's not what I meant," he replied.

"I know," she said as she took a seat on the edge of the bed.

"What's going on?" he asked more sincerely.

"Seeing you the other day made me realize something that has been in the back of my mind for a while now," she said.

"And what's that?" Tim asked.

"That I made a mistake," she said, looking up at him.

He let out a sigh and put his face in his hands. He moved his hands up through his hair and sat back in the chair.

"I tried telling you this when you were making your decision," he said.

"I know, but there were different factors then," she said, looking down at her stomach.

Tim followed her gaze and then looked back up at her face.

"I told you we could have figured it out," he said.

"You wanted me to get an abortion," she responded defensively.

"I didn't want you to get one. I was just telling you it was an option. I'm sorry if it came off that way," he said.

"It doesn't matter now," Sarah replied as she looked away.

There was a moment of silence between them.

"What do you want?" Tim asked.

"It's not that easy," she answered.

"I understand that. But what do you want?" he asked again.

"I want you," she replied.

She returned her gaze to Tim's face. He was staring at her intently. Before she knew it, he was on top of her, kissing her passionately. Her back was against the bed and his tongue was in her mouth. She could feel his penis growing beneath his jeans. He suddenly pulled away.

"I'm sorry. We can't do this," he said as he moved back toward the chair.

"I know," she said, sitting back up on the bed.

"You're married," he said.

"I know," she said again.

"Jesus Christ, Sarah. Why couldn't you have figured this out sooner?" he asked.

"I don't know," she replied.

"Like, this really complicates things," he said.

"I know," she said once again.

"So what are you going to do?" he asked.

"What do you mean?" she asked.

"Are you going to get a divorce?" he asked.

"That's definitely something we will have to talk about. But I don't want to hurt him," she said.

"You're already hurting him," he replied.

She looked at the floor again.

"I know," she said.

Tim stood up from the chair and went and sat next to Sarah on the bed. He wrapped his arm around her waist. She laid her head on his shoulder.

"I wish I had a time machine," she said.

"Me too," he replied.

"So what do you think Charlie was dressed up for?" Sarah asked, changing the subject.

"He had a job interview," Tim answered.

Sarah lifted her head up and looked at him confused.

"How do you know?" she asked.

"He told me," he responded.

"When?" she asked.

"When he called me today. He asked me if I knew about anything going on with you, so I told him you thought he was cheating on you," he replied.

"You what?" Sarah asked angrily.

"Hey, don't get mad at me. You disappeared and we were both worried about you. I didn't know anything then and I was trying to help," he said.

Sarah was silent for a moment as she realized he was right.

"What did he say?" she asked.

"This is really something you should be talking about with him," Tim replied.

"OK, but he's not here. So can you give me the synopsis of it?" she asked.

"Basically, his health insurance from the military is ending and he needs to find a job so you have health insurance," he answered.

"And he didn't think of telling me any of this why?" she asked.

"You'll have to ask him. But I'm sure he didn't want to stress you out any more than you've already been," he replied.

"That makes sense. It's a lame excuse, but it makes sense," she said.

"Like I said, you need to talk to him," Tim said.

"I know. And I will," she said.

They sat there in silence as they both processed the information they had just learned. Tim was ecstatic to know Sarah wanted to be with him. But at the same time, he knew it would be a while before they would be able to be together. He wasn't going to do anything while she was still married to Charlie. And he didn't know if she would go through with the divorce.

He knew Sarah cared for Charlie. He was her best friend. They have a bond Tim would never understand. He was just starting to get over Sarah when she contacted him on Saturday. She broke his heart and then a month later reappeared. He knew he had to take all of this with a grain of salt, but he couldn't help but be hopeful.

Sarah knew what she wanted. But she also knew she had been through some traumatic experiences lately and she didn't want that to play a role in her decision-making. She knew she wasn't going to get her answers sitting in a hotel room in Kalamazoo. She needed to talk to Charlie and tell him how she felt, even if it would hurt him. He deserved to know the truth, she thought.

"Do you want to get dinner?" Tim asked.

His voice brought her back to the present.

"I'm sorry. What did you say?" she asked.

He let out a light laugh.

"I asked if you wanted to get dinner," he said.

"Oh. Yes, please. I'm starving," she said, realizing she hadn't had a meal all day.

"Perfect. There's this brewery right down the road that has really good food," Tim said.

"That sounds good to me," Sarah replied.

The two of them left the hotel and began walking to the brewery. On the way there, Tim grabbed Sarah's hand as they walked. She smiled up at him and gave his hand a light squeeze. It was nice to hold his hand again, she thought to herself. She held it the whole way to the restaurant.

They were seated right away when they got there. After reading the menu, they both placed their orders and waited for their food to arrive. There was an awkward silence as neither of them knew what to say. They both knew they wanted the same thing, but the journey to that outcome was long.

"So what do you think you're going to do?" Tim asked, interrupting the silence.

"I'm going to have to talk to Charlie," she answered.

"Yup, that would be a good idea," he said laughing.

Sarah gave him a slight smile. She missed his laugh. She missed him. She missed everything about him.

The way he touched her. The way he tasted. She knew she had to find a way to be with him again.

"I want you, Tim," she said.

"We've established that," he said smiling.

"No, like I want you. I want all of you. I want to be with you," she confirmed.

"I know," he said. "But how are you going to make that happen?"

"I'm going to have to divorce Charlie," she replied.

"And you're OK with that?" he asked.

"I have to be," she said.

Tim reached across the table and gently grabbed her hand. He caressed the back of it with his thumb.

"I know that's not going to be easy for you. I know how much he means to you," he said.

"But you mean more," Sarah responded.

Tim smiled. He didn't know if that was true, but he liked the thought of it. In the hospital, he told Sarah he loved her. Back then, she told him she couldn't say those words back to him. He didn't know if that was because she had already decided to marry Charlie because they were having a baby together or if she just didn't reciprocate those feelings. His thoughts were interrupted by the arrival of their food.

They ate in silence for the most part, except for some small talk about how their food tasted. Afterward, Tim paid for the meal and they walked back to the hotel. They didn't hold hands. Tim stopped on the sidewalk outside of the entrance.

"You're not going to come up?" Sarah asked confused.

"I probably shouldn't," he answered.

"I would really like you to," she said.

"You know nothing can happen between us," he said.

"I know," she said.

Tim eyed her suspiciously.

"You promise you won't try to seduce me?" he asked playfully.

Sarah laughed out loud. She held up three fingers. "Scout's honor," she said.

"OK. I can come up for a little bit then," he said.

He followed Sarah into the hotel and up to her room. It was about 8:30 p.m. Sarah noticed Tim looked tired.

"You can stay the night," she said.

"I should probably stay at my brother's," he replied.

"Does he know you're in town?" she asked.

"No, but he won't mind," he answered.

"Please stay," she said.

Tim looked at her face. He could sense her sadness. He knew a little of what she had been going through, but he would never be able to fully understand. Despite everything, she looked as beautiful as ever to him. He didn't want to see her hurting.

He approached her and wrapped his arms around her. She held him back and pressed her head into his chest. She didn't want to let go. She knew she had to find a way to be with him.

"I'll stay," he said.

Sarah lifted her head up and smiled at him.

"Really?" she asked excitedly.

"Yes," he answered. "But you should tell Charlie."

Sarah pulled away from the hug and looked at Tim confused.

"I already told him I needed a few days away," she said.

"I mean that I'm here," Tim said.

"He doesn't know you came?" she asked.

"No," he replied.

"What did you tell him?" she asked.

"I told him you were OK, and you would reach out to him when you were ready," he said.

"Oh," she said.

"You should tell him," he insisted.

"I'm already going to talk to him when I get back. Isn't that enough?" she asked.

"Sarah, he's your best friend. He probably has no idea you're about to drop this bombshell on him. Don't you think he deserves a little heads up?" he asked.

"Yeah, you're right," she said.

She went and sat on the edge of the bed with her cell phone in her hand. She knew Charlie deserved a phone call, but she couldn't bring herself to talk to him yet. Instead, she decided a text message would suffice.

I just wanted to let you know Tim is with me. He came to make sure I'm OK, which I am. He is spending the night, but nothing is going to happen between us. I wouldn't do that to you. I just wanted you to know. I will see you when I get home, the text read.

She waited for him to immediately call her, but he didn't. A few minutes went by and there was no response. She turned and looked at Tim. He shrugged his shoulders.

"At least you told him," he said.

"I feel bad," she replied.

"I can leave," he said.

"I don't want you to," she said.

She rolled over on her side and patted the bed next to her, motioning for Tim to join her. He laid down on the opposite side of the bed, keeping his distance. She scooted closer to him. He rolled onto his back. She laid her head on his chest and draped her arm across his stomach. He kept one arm by his side and the other behind his head. They fell asleep.

11

Sarah woke up the next morning and checked her phone. There was still no reply from Charlie. She thought about texting him again, but decided against it. She would talk to him when she got home, which she determined would be that day. She turned back over and saw Tim still sleeping.

She smiled. It was nice to sleep in his arms again, she thought. Even though nothing happened between them, she was happy he stayed. She pressed her body up against his back and held him. He rolled over to face her.

"Good morning," he said with a smile.

"Good morning," she said, smiling back.

"Are you ready to head back to Muncie yet?" he asked.

"No, but I probably should," she replied.

"Let me take you out to breakfast first," he said.

"OK," she said excitedly.

The two of them got ready and then checked out of the hotel. Tim helped Sarah put her bags in her car before the two of them walked to his vehicle. He drove them to the Breakfast Nook. It was Tim's favorite restaurant in Kalamazoo. They served breakfast fresh from the farm every single day, except Sundays. That was "God's day," and the restaurant was closed.

Tim ordered the Farmer's Special, which included two eggs made to order, two pieces of bacon, two sausage links, two slices of toast, and two pancakes. He ordered his eggs scrambled.

"That's a lot of food," Sarah said.

"It's so worth it though," he replied.

"OK. I'll have the same. But make my eggs sunny side up, please," she told the waiter.

"You got it. That will be right out," the waiter responded.

"So this is your favorite restaurant?" Sarah asked, looking around.

There was old farm equipment hanging on the walls all the way around the restaurant. A distressed sign hung from the ceiling that read "Farm Fresh." It was a quaint restaurant and the floor looked like it hadn't been swept in days. Tim read Sarah's mind.

"Wait until you try the food. I promise you won't be disappointed," he said.

"It's just breakfast food," she said.

Tim gasped.

"You take that back right now," he said jokingly.

Sarah laughed.

"What?" she asked.

"This is the best breakfast in the whole world," he exclaimed.

"OK. If you say so," she said.

"Just wait," he said.

A short while later, the waiter returned with two orders of the Farmer's Special. It looked pretty good, Sarah thought. She looked up and noticed Tim was staring at her intently, waiting to see her reaction after her first bite. She picked up a slice of bacon. It was nice and crispy, just the way she liked it. She took a bite.

"Oh my God," she exclaimed.

"I told you," Tim replied.

"That's the best bacon I've ever had," she said.

"I know," he said.

"What do they put on it?" she asked.

"I don't know, but it's amazing," he said.

"Mhm," she agreed.

She finished the slice of bacon and moved on to one of the sausage links. She placed it in her mouth and began to chew. The juices from the meat released onto her tongue.

"Mmm. So good," she moaned.

Tim laughed.

"What did I tell you?" he asked.

"I will never doubt you again," she replied.

"Good," he said victoriously.

They finished their breakfast and then got back into Tim's car. Sarah made him promise to bring her back there one day, which he agreed. A short while later, they arrived at Sarah's car.

"Are you going to be OK driving back by yourself?" he asked.

He knew she just recently started driving again after the crash and he was worried about her traveling that far alone.

"I'll be fine," she said.

"Just call me if you need anything, OK?" he replied.

"OK," she said.

Tim leaned over and gave her a quick kiss on the cheek.

"I mean it. Anything," he said.

"Thank you," she said.

"For what?" he asked confused.

"For driving here. For staying with me. For breakfast. For everything," she replied.

He grabbed her hand.

"It was no problem at all," he said.

She smiled at him.

"We'll talk later, OK?" he said.

"OK," she said.

Sarah exited his car and got into hers. She checked her phone again. There was still no reply from Charlie. She decided to call him to let him know she was on her way home. It went straight to voicemail. Charlie never turned his phone off. She tried calling again. Voicemail. She decided against leaving him a message.

She turned her car on and began the three-hour trek home. She tried to plan out her conversation with Charlie in her head, but she kept getting distracted by images of Tim sleeping next to her in bed. She craved his touch. Tim had touched her in a way she had never experienced before. She longed to feel that sensation again.

She felt herself becoming wet at the thought of him. She shook the images of Tim's naked body out of her head and turned the radio louder. She found herself singing along to "Bang Bang" by Nicki Minaj. Before she realized it, she was taking the Muncie exit.

She completely zoned out and could not remember the last three hours.

She was 10 minutes from home and had no idea what she was going to say to her husband. She only knew she had to ask for a divorce and that wasn't going to be an easy conversation to have. With all of her heart, she didn't want to hurt Charlie. He was her best friend and had been there for her through everything. She loved him, but not in the same way he loved her. She knew she would never be fully happy with him.

They would be better off as friends. But she didn't know if their friendship would survive this. She had put him through a lot during their 20-plus years of friendship, but nothing as heartbreaking as divorce. Her heart began to ache for Charlie. She thought about staying with him to save him the heartbreak, but she knew that wasn't fair to either of them. He deserved to be with someone who loved him as much as he loved her, and she deserved the same. She hoped he would understand.

She pulled into their driveway and his car was gone. She entered the house looking for him, but he wasn't there. However, all of his stuff was. That's a good sign, she thought. She tried calling him again, but his phone was still off. She thought about calling his parents to see if they had heard from him, but she didn't want to let them know they were having problems if Charlie hadn't talked to them.

She unpacked her bag and waited on the couch for him to come home. An hour had passed. Then two. The next thing she knew, it was 5 p.m. and he still wasn't home. She tried his cell again. Voicemail. She decided to leave a message this time.

"Hey. It's me. I've been trying to call you all day, but your phone is off. I'm at home and you're not here. I'm starting to get worried. Please call me back," she said in the message.

She went into the kitchen to make herself something to eat. She opened the fridge and stared blankly inside. Nothing sounded good to her. She realized she wasn't hungry. But she knew she should eat. She hadn't had any sustenance since her breakfast with Tim. Man, that bacon was good, she thought.

She grabbed a couple grapes out of the fridge and popped them into her mouth. That will suffice, she decided. She walked back into the living room and looked out the front window. Charlie's car was still gone. She wondered where he was.

She went upstairs and picked up her copy of *A Summer Affair* by Elin Hilderbrand. She realized she never finished reading it. She found the title fitting of her current situation, even though she wasn't technically having an affair with Tim. If an emotional affair was a thing, she was having that, she decided.

She fell asleep while reading. She was awoken about an hour later by Charlie gently shaking her shoulder. He was perched on the edge of her bed. She looked up at him. She couldn't read his face. She couldn't tell if he was confused, hurt or angry. Probably a combination of all three, she decided.

"Hey," she said.

"Hey," he replied.

There was no emotion in his voice. It remained flat. There was silence between them.

"Where were you?" she finally asked curiously.

"I got a job. The interview was yesterday, and they asked me to start immediately. So today was my first day," he answered.

"Oh," Sarah said, looking down at the floor.

"It was a good distraction," he said.

She looked back at Charlie's face. She could sense the pain now.

"I'm sor...," she started to say but she was interrupted by Charlie.

"No, let me. I'm sorry I didn't tell you. I didn't want to stress you out. You have been through so much and I didn't want to add to any of that. I should have told you. I understand that now. And I'm sorry. But I want you to know, I would never, ever cheat on you," he said.

"I know," she replied.

"You do?" he asked.

"Yes," she responded.

"But, I thought...," he started.

"I did think you were cheating on me. I never really believed it. I know you and I know you wouldn't do that. But I think part of me wanted it to be true because it would have made this conversation easier," she said.

"What conversation?" he asked confused.

Sarah realized he had no idea what she was about to tell him. This was coming completely out of the blue. He didn't have time to prepare. She grabbed his hand softly.

"We can't be married," she said.

"But we are married," he replied, still confused.

"I know. But we can't be anymore," she said.

"I don't understand," he said.

"This isn't working out," she said.

"Is this because of the baby? Is it something I did? I can fix it. Just let me know what I did, and I can fix it," he responded.

"There's nothing to fix. It's nothing you did. We never should have gotten married. It was for all the wrong reasons," she said.

"But, I love you," he said with a lump in his throat.

Sarah could see the tears pooling on the bottom of his eyelids.

"I know. And I love you too, but not in the same way you love me," she said.

The tears began to drip down his face. Sarah's heart was breaking for him. She never wanted to hurt him. She wanted to immediately take her words back to save him from this heartbreak, but she knew she couldn't do that.

"I don't understand. I thought everything was going good," he said.

"It was. But this was never meant to be, you and me. We're better off as friends," she said.

"But… we belong together," he said, quoting their song.

Sarah picked up on the reference and gave him a half-smile.

"I am really sorry, Charlie. I never wanted to hurt you. I know how you feel about me, and I wish so much I felt the same. But I don't. And there's nothing I can do about that," she said.

"You could try," he replied.

"I have tried. And this just isn't working out for me," she said.

Charlie looked into her eyes. He could see his reflection in her irises. Tear streams stained his face.

Sarah reached her hand up and wiped the wetness from his cheek. The feeling of her soft hand on his face sent a chill down his spine.

He loved this woman more than he had ever loved anything in his life. He believed one day she would feel the same way for him, and he thought that time had come. But he was wrong. So wrong. He felt lost and hopeless. He didn't know what to do.

"Is this because of Tim?" he asked angrily.

"No. This isn't because of anybody. You deserve to be with someone who loves you as much as you love her. And I can't keep pretending that's me. As much as I wish it was, it's not," Sarah answered.

"I don't want anyone else," Charlie replied somberly.

"I'm sorry, Charlie," she said.

"Can't we talk about this?" he asked as tears began to pour down his face again.

"There's nothing to talk about. I can't force myself to love you the way you want me to," she replied.

Her heart was breaking. She thought saying goodbye to her dad would be the hardest thing she ever had to do. But in this moment, she knew she was crushing Charlie's heart. And that hurt her more than losing her dad. She knew she was losing her best friend in the process.

"I should go," Charlie said after what felt like an eternity of silence.

She didn't want him to leave. She wanted to hug him and take all of his pain away. But she knew she couldn't do that.

"OK," she responded understandingly.

He stood up from the bed and looked around the room.

"I'll uh, come back for my stuff later," he said.

Sarah nodded. She didn't want Charlie to move out. She had gotten use to him being there. She didn't want to be alone in her house because she knew it would make her miss her dad more. But she knew he couldn't stay.

Charlie turned around and walked out of her room. A single tear dripped down Sarah's cheek. She knew she just watched her best friend walk out of her life. She wasn't ready to mourn another loss so soon, but she knew she had to.

12

A week after the tough conversation with Sarah, Charlie moved all of his things out of her house and back into his apartment. Luckily, his lease wasn't up so he had a place to go. He hadn't told his parents about them getting a divorce because it still didn't feel real to him. He kept hoping it was a horrible nightmare he was going to wake up from.

But he wasn't sleeping. This was his life. And the woman he had loved since she was a little girl did not love him back, at least in the way he wished. He knew Sarah cared for him, but as a friend. He wished he had never proposed. He wished he could go back in time to when he came home from the military and take back the moment he confessed his feelings to her.

After thinking about that for a moment, he was happy he couldn't time travel. He enjoyed their time together. He got to experience her body, which was incredible, he thought. They made life together. And then lost that life, he thought sadly.

That was the saddest day of his life, he realized. Not when Sarah told him she wanted a divorce, but when they found out they had lost their baby. He was looking forward to being a father and seeing Sarah grow as a mother. He wondered if they would have stayed married if she never had a miscarriage.

It didn't matter, he decided. She only married him because she was pregnant, and because she needed health insurance, he added. If they remained married, it wouldn't have been for the right reasons, he thought. He was beginning to understand Sarah's decision. He still didn't like it, but he was starting to understand it.

After that first week, Charlie immersed himself into his work. It was hard labor, and it kept his mind off of the heartbreak he was feeling. He was the first to volunteer for every overtime opportunity. He began working six and seven days a week. Some days he would put in 16 hours.

He was so exhausted when he got home, he would collapse on the couch and sleep there for the night. He would wake up, shower, eat, work, sleep, and repeat. That was it. He didn't have the energy to think about Sarah. He felt pain, but only the physical pain from the extensive labors of the construction industry. He was numb to everything else.

As for Sarah, she had returned to work at the bookstore in the middle of October. She was happy to learn Cindy had taken an internship and was no longer working at the store. Cindy had been replaced by a young, red-haired BSU freshman named Stella. Stella wore black, large-rimmed glasses and had freckles painted across her face. She was quiet and didn't ask Sarah personal questions, which Sarah appreciated.

The owner of the bookstore said Sarah could ease herself back into working full-time, but Sarah jumped right in. She wanted the distraction. She didn't want to think about Charlie or their impending divorce. She had the papers sitting on her kitchen table at home waiting to be filled out. She wasn't sure what she was waiting for.

Even though she was still covered under Charlie's health insurance for the time-being, she stopped going to physical therapy. She knew it was going to happen eventually once the divorce was finalized, but she had improved enough where she could function on her own. She could also do most of the exercises at home, she decided. The exercises kept her busy and kept her mind off of Tim.

She hadn't seen Tim since she left Kalamazoo. They texted a few times, but both decided she should take some time to focus on herself before they even talked about getting back together. It was hard for her not to see him or Charlie. She felt so alone, but she knew she had to figure out what she really wanted before she hurt anyone else.

She had been spending a lot of time at her Aunt Susan's house to try to avoid the gaping hole she felt inside her. Plus, Susan reminded her of her dad. It was like a little piece of him was still there. Susan was the only family she had left.

Susan never married and Sarah couldn't remember her ever dating anyone. She never brought anyone around, not even a friend. She wondered if her aunt had friends. Suddenly, she began to feel sorry for her aunt. She realized she didn't check in on her as often as she should. She wondered if her aunt felt lonely too.

"I've been thinking I should take a trip," Susan said over dinner one evening.

Sarah was caught off guard. Her aunt never went anywhere. She wasn't even sure if she had ever been outside of Indiana.

"What?" she asked.

"A trip. And I'd like you to come with me," Susan answered.

"Where do you want to go?" Sarah asked.

"Asia," she responded.

Sarah had never been to Asia. It was her dream to visit Thailand, but she didn't have the money or the time for that right now.

"Aunt Susan, I just started working again. I can't take the time off for a trip like that," she said.

"Quit your job. Come with me. It will be an adventure," Susan said excitedly.

Sarah wondered where this was coming from. She had never seen this side of her aunt before.

"You want me to quit my job?" she asked.

"Yes. You can always find another one when you get back," Susan said.

"When we get back, you mean," Sarah said.

"Sure," her aunt responded, breaking her gaze from Sarah's face.

Sarah put her fork and knife down on her plate.

"Aunt Susan, what's going on?" she asked concerned.

"It's nothing," Susan replied, not making eye contact.

"Sue," Sarah said seriously.

Her aunt hated being called Sue. She looked up at Sarah with spite in her eyes.

"What's going on?" Sarah asked again.

Her aunt let out a dramatic sigh and slung herself into the back of her chair.

"I have a friend in Taiwan. He's not doing well, and he wants me to visit before he goes," she said somberly.

"I'm so sorry, Aunt Susan. How much time does he have left?" Sarah asked.

"Not long," she answered.

"Is he a good friend?" Sarah asked.

"The best," she answered.

"I don't remember you ever mentioning him before," Sarah replied.

"Because he's my secret letter lover," Susan said

"Letter lover?" Sarah asked.

"We've been writing each other sexual letters for decades. Descriptions of what we would like to do to each other once we finally meet," she responded with a smirk.

Sarah could not believe what she was hearing. She thought her aunt was so boring and now she was learning she had been basically sexting a stranger for decades.

"Wait. So you've never met?" she asked.

"Nope," Susan replied.

"Do you know what he looks like?" she asked.

"Only through photos," Susan answered.

"Do you have one? May I see?" Sarah asked intrigued.

"Of course. Let me go find one," she answered.

Susan stood up from the table and walked into the other room. Sarah could hear her fumbling through her desk. She sat back in her chair dumbfounded. She couldn't believe her aunt had been living this secret life. She suddenly wanted to know everything about this mystery man. Was he married? Did he have kids? How did this start? She had so many questions.

Then she felt a ping of sadness. Her aunt never married. She said they had been corresponding for decades. She wondered if her aunt was in love with this mystery man and that's why she never dated. How lonely she must have been all of this time, Sarah thought.

And now this man was dying, and her aunt never got to meet him. That thought broke Sarah's heart. She decided she would do whatever she had to to make sure her aunt meets him before that happens. Her aunt walked back into the kitchen with a pile of old photos and letters. She pulled up a chair next to Sarah and sat down.

"This is the first photo he ever sent me. He was in his young-20s here," she said, holding up a black-and-white photograph.

"Wow. He's stunning," Sarah said impressed.

Sarah grabbed the photo so she could get a closer look. This was not what she had been expecting at all. He was tall, dark, and had the sexiest jawline she had ever seen. His muscles were bulging through his T-shirt. She would have fallen in love with this hunk too, she decided.

"What's his name?" Sarah asked.

"Chun-chieh," Susan replied. "But I call him Chun."

"Chun-chieh," Sarah repeated to herself.

"And this is the last photo I received from him about a month ago," Susan said, holding up another photograph.

The second photo was in color and it showed a much older man. He must be in his late 60s or early 70s, Sarah decided. He had wrinkles plastered across his face and appeared much shorter than he had decades before. His jawline was no longer chiseled, but he aged well, Sarah thought.

"How did this start?" Sarah asked.

"Well, about 40-some years ago there was a column in the newspaper asking for pen pals to write letters to residents in our sister city in Taiwan. I was a young, single woman in my 20s. So I thought it would be kind of sexy to have a foreign pen pal. I signed up and we hit it off right away. And we kept it going all these years later," she said fondly.

"And you never thought about going to visit him or him coming here?" she asked.

"I definitely thought about it. On more than one occasion too. But I've never flown before. And what we have in our letters is so perfect, what if real-life didn't match? I didn't want to ruin what we had, or have I should say," Susan replied.

"Wow. That's incredible. I had no clue," Sarah said.

"No one did. He's been my little secret this whole time," she said.

"Is he married?" Sarah asked.

"He was. His wife died about five years ago," she answered.

"You wrote letters to a married man?" Sarah asked confrontationally and excitedly.

"There was a period where the letters slowed down, but they never completely stopped," Susan responded.

"This is amazing, Aunt Susan. I cannot believe you have been keeping this a secret this whole time," Sarah said.

"To be honest, it feels good to finally tell someone," she said.

"So when do you want to go?" Sarah asked.

"We leave Saturday. I already bought our plane tickets," Susan responded.

Sarah's mouth dropped open.

"That's not enough notice for me to tell my work," she protested.

"Honey, you've been off work for several weeks. I think they've learned to manage without you," her aunt said ruder than she meant.

"That's not the point," Sarah whined.

There was silence between them as Sarah glared at her aunt.

"So you just assumed I would say yes?" Sarah asked annoyed.

"Of course. You're you. You can't turn down a trip. And you don't even have to pay for this one," Susan replied with a grin.

She knew her niece and she knew she was right.

"Maybe that's true. But this was super shady, Sue," Sarah said with a smirk.

Susan rolled her eyes.

"Whatever. So are you going to make me go alone or what?" she asked.

"Of course not. You've never been outside of Indiana. You wouldn't survive in a foreign country by yourself," Sarah answered.

"Perfect," Susan said.

"I have one question though," Sarah began.

"What's that?" Susan asked.

"What am I going to do while you two, you know," she hinted.

"Oh honey," Susan said laughing. "I bought you a flight to Thailand shortly after we get there. But that's assuming everything goes good and he's not catfishing me."

Sarah let out a laugh.

"How do you even know what catfishing is?" she asked.

"I'm hip. I know what the kids say nowadays," Susan replied.

Sarah laughed harder as she pictured her aunt sitting on the couch binge-watching trash reality shows. Then she realized her aunt said Thailand.

"Wait. You bought me a plane ticket to Thailand?" she asked.

"Isn't that where you've always wanted to go?" Susan asked.

"Yes, but…," she began.

She didn't know what to say. Thailand was her dream trip, but she never thought she would be going this soon or in this way. She was used to traveling by herself, she actually preferred it. But something about this trip felt off to her.

"I don't know what to say," she said.

"You don't have to say anything. You've been through a lot this year and you deserve this. Besides, I think this will be a good opportunity for you to clear your head. Truly find yourself and figure out what you want with your life," Susan said.

Sarah thought about her aunt's words. She was right. She needed time for herself. She needed to reflect on what she truly wanted before she could be happy with Tim. Tim, she thought. Ever since their first date, she always pictured the two of them going to Thailand together. She wondered if he would be upset if she went without him.

It didn't matter, she decided. It was too late. The flights were purchased. He would have to understand, she thought. She pictured herself snorkeling at Railay Beach, strolling through the halls of the Grand Palace, and observing the ancient Buddha statues in Ayutthaya. She would visit elephants, and purchase food from floating markets, and bathe in waterfalls.

Susan could tell her niece was lost deep in her own thoughts.

"There is one catch though," she said.

Sarah looked up at her aunt with concern.

"What's that?" she asked.

"The flight is one-way. You will have to book your return flight home. I didn't know how long you wanted to stay. So I figured it would be best to leave that up to you," she said.

Sarah's eyes widened. She never had an open-ended trip before. This brought new excitement to her upcoming adventure. She could stay as long as she wanted and do whatever she wanted.

"Aunt Susan, you're the best," she exclaimed.

13

That Saturday, Susan and Sarah drove a rental car to Indianapolis International Airport where they boarded their first flight. Susan had never flown before and was nervous about the whole ordeal. Sarah had her take some allergy medicine with two shots of tequila before the flight. The plan was to have her sleep through most of it.

But that plan backfired. The tequila made Susan frisky and she kept flirting with the male flight attendant, who was obviously gay. Sarah was so embarrassed. She had her headphones in and pretended she didn't know her aunt.

They landed at Dallas/Fort Worth International Airport where they had a two-hour layover before their next leg. By that time, the tequila had worn off and Susan was becoming cranky. She was mad at Sarah for ignoring her on the previous flight. She was clearly becoming tired, Sarah thought. She hoped that meant her aunt would sleep on the next flight so she could as well.

They had about a 13-hour flight from Dallas to Japan, where their last layover was. Sarah was hoping to sleep on that flight so she would be refreshed and ready for the day when they arrived in Taiwan. The plan was for her to spend the first night with her aunt to make sure Chun-chieh wasn't a catfish. Sarah laughed at the thought of her aunt being catfished by a Taiwanese man.

Then Sarah would leave her aunt behind and head to Thailand for as long as her heart desired. She didn't have much time to plan with her aunt springing the trip on her last minute, but she was able to book a hostel just outside of downtown Bangkok for her first three nights. After that, she would head to Phuket for a few days of relaxation in paradise.

Her thoughts of her trip were interrupted by the sound of Susan snoring. Sarah looked over at her aunt and saw her hunched over in an airport chair with her head rolled back and her mouth wide open. She was snoring so loud. Sarah looked around to see if anyone was staring at them, but everyone was lost in their own world. They either had headphones in, were staring blankly at their cell phone screens, or snoozing themselves.

That was one thing Sarah always enjoyed about traveling. You could be surrounded by hundreds of people, and none of them pay any attention to you. It's not that way in Muncie. You walk past someone on the street and they say hello. Everyone is friendly back home. Sarah doesn't mind that, but it's nice being ignored one in a while, she thought.

She checked the time on her phone and saw it was about a half an hour until they boarded their next flight. She leaned over and nudged her aunt awake.

Susan sleepily opened her eyes and looked around confused.

"We're going to be boarding soon. We have to get to our gate," Sarah said.

Susan continued looking around the airport.

"Where are we?" she asked sleepily.

"The Dallas airport. We're about to fly to Japan," Sarah answered.

"Chun-chieh?" Susan asked.

"Chun-chieh is in Taiwan. But yes, we're going to meet him," Sarah laughed.

That seemed to have woken Susan up. She craned her neck to the side until she heard a crack. Then she let out a relieving sigh.

"Are you ready?" Sarah asked.

Susan nodded her head. The two of them gathered up their luggage and walked to their gate. After boarding, Susan was too excited to fall back asleep. Sarah let her have the window seat so she could see the ocean. It amazed her that her aunt had never seen an ocean before. She wondered how someone could go their whole life without seeing the world.

After the plane took off, Sarah showed her aunt how to work the in-flight entertainment. There were an assortment of movies and TV shows to watch, as well as games to play. Susan seemed enthralled with all of the different options. Sarah used that opportunity to get some sleep. She woke up once for the complimentary meal and then quickly fell back asleep after eating.

Hours later, Sarah woke up to the pilot making his descent announcement. They would land in 35 minutes. The local time was 8:32 a.m. The landing was rougher than Sarah was used to, but Susan didn't seem to mind. She was too excited to be on the same continent as Chun-chieh.

Their layover in Japan was short. They only had time to use the restroom before their flight began to board. It was about a four-hour flight from Tokyo to Taipei, where Chun-chieh was going to pick them up. After takeoff, Sarah looked over at her aunt. Susan looked like she hadn't slept in days. The bags under her eyes were dark and her hair was a frizzy mess.

Sarah encouraged her aunt to try to get some sleep so she would have energy for her first day with Chun-chieh. But Susan was too excited. She couldn't sleep. Her heart was racing. She kept replaying different conversations in her head that she had been waiting to have with this man she had fallen in love with many moons ago.

Besides excitement, there was a lot weighing on Susan's mind. She regretted not making the trip sooner. Not moving to Taiwan when he asked nearly 40-years prior. They could have had a beautiful life together, she thought. Instead, he married someone else and had two children with her. Chia-Ling was her name, which Susan learned meant beautiful.

She didn't know if Chia-Ling was beautiful. She never asked about her, and Chun-chieh never mentioned her in his letters, besides the letter announcing he was getting married. She remembered the heartbreak she felt when she received that letter.

She was devastated. She vowed to end their correspondence then. He wrote her a few more letters after that, but they went unanswered. Susan was too devastated to reply. Then about six months after the initial letter announcing his nuptials, she wrote him back. The letter was short.

Chun,
I'm still mad. But I can't stop thinking about you.
Love always,
Suzie

That was all she wrote, but it was enough to continue their letter affair. Chun-chieh loved Susan, but he was lonely and he needed a wife. He needed someone to do the cooking and cleaning while he worked. He was a traditionalist. Plus, he had needs that Susan just couldn't meet over letter-writing.

He told her he was a man and his hand would not suffice any longer. She was furious, but she understood. She couldn't expect him to stay single forever, especially when she didn't have any plans to go visit him. But she always remained faithful to him. She never ventured out for a date with another man, because she knew her heart had a home all the way across the world.

Now here she was, decades later, finally going to meet the man she had been dreaming about almost every night. Susan had recently been diagnosed with cancer and was told she didn't have long to live. Unlike her brother, there weren't any treatment options available to her. She told her niece Chun-chieh was the one who was ill because she didn't want to worry her.

She also thought if she told Sarah it was her, she wouldn't go on the trip. Sarah would insist on them staying home and taking care of her. And Susan just couldn't have that. She needed to see this man before she died, even if the trip killed her. It was her dying wish.

The pilot began to make his descent announcement. They were a half hour away from landing. The local time was 1:47 p.m. Susan's heart was beating faster as the minutes dwindled until she was finally going to meet the man who captured her heart all those years prior.

Sarah looked over at her aunt. The bags under her eyes were still prominent and her hair was still frizzy. Chun-chieh was supposed to pick them up at the airport. She couldn't let her aunt look like this the first time she met the possible love of her life, Sarah decided. She reached into her purse and pulled out a stick of concealer. She started dabbing it under Susan's eyes.

"What are you doing?" she asked, caught off guard.

"You're going to meet Chun-chieh for the first time in a little bit. Don't you want to look presentable?" Sarah asked.

"Do you really think he's going to care what I look like?" she asked.

"He might. I'm sure he has this picture-perfect image of you in his head. You don't want to let him down, do you?" Sarah replied.

"I guess you're right," Susan said.

Sarah continued dabbing the concealer under her aunt's eyes. Then she rubbed it in with her index finger.

"Much better," she said. "As for your hair, you're on your own."

"What's wrong with my hair?" Susan asked offended.

Sarah let out a laugh. Susan squinted her eyes at her and reached into her own purse. She pulled out a small compact mirror and opened it up. She held it in front of her face and moved her head so she could examine her hair.

"Oh my God," she said. "What am I going to do?"

"Do you have a hat?" Sarah asked.

"A big sun hat in my carry-on, but wouldn't that look weird?" she asked.

"No, that's perfect. There's plenty of beaches around," Sarah replied.

Susan gave her niece a half-smile. She was happy Sarah was with her on this adventure. She knew she wouldn't have boarded the plane without her. And seeing Chun-chieh was something she needed to do. She felt it in her heart. But now that the moment was approaching, her nerves began to take over.

What if he didn't speak English very well, she wondered. He could write it, but she never actually spoke to him. Even with the technology of cell phones and video calls, their relationship was maintained by the traditional art of letter writing. Susan found it romantic and didn't want to change that. Afterall, those letters were all she had. They were something tangible she could hold onto at night when the loneliness crept in.

"Everything is going to be OK," Sarah said, as if she were reading her aunt's thoughts.

"I know," Susan replied, squeezing her niece's hand for support.

Everything was going to be OK, she thought. Then the plane landed and as soon as the wheels hit the runway, all of her nerves disappeared. For the first time in her life, she was in the same country as her love. She was ready to dart off the plane and run into Chun-chieh's arms. But she had to wait for the pilot to turn off the seatbelt light, and for everyone ahead of her to exit the plane first. She began to tap her feet on the ground as she grew more impatient.

"Soon," Sarah reassured her.

After what felt like an eternity, Susan and Sarah were walking down the gangway toward the airport. Sarah looked at her aunt and saw the biggest smile on her face. Susan almost had a glow about her. Sarah had never seen her aunt look so happy before. She was happy she was there to experience that life-changing moment with her. Susan looked back at her niece.

"Thank you for coming," she said.

"Of course. I wouldn't miss this," Sarah responded.

They followed the signs in the airport to the baggage claim area. Upon entering the room, Sarah's eyes darted around looking for Chun-Chieh. She only briefly saw a current photo of him, but she thought she might be able to pick him out from the crowd. Her gaze was interrupted by her aunt's voice.

"Oh, my sweet heavenly father," Susan said.

Sarah looked at her aunt and followed her gaze. Standing 25-feet in front of them was a man who appeared to be in his late 60s. Chun-chieh. He was about 5'9" and had a slim build. He had pure silver hair and a matching beard. He was more handsome in person, Sarah thought. He was holding a bouquet of nearly 50 red roses, and a sign that read *My love, Susan.*

Susan dropped her belongings and ran toward him. He placed the sign and roses on the ground, and picked Susan up into a hug, swinging her in a circle. Their lips met immediately, like a magnetic force pulling them together. Sarah had never witnessed a more passionate kiss. She began to blush. She looked around the airport to see if anyone else was watching this historic moment, but everyone else was too caught up in their own world.

Sarah didn't want to interrupt their special moment, but she also felt awkward standing by herself. She leaned down and picked up her aunt's belongings and slowly walked toward the lovebirds. As she approached, Chun-chieh placed Susan back on her feet and extended his hand to Sarah.

"You must be Sarah," he said with perfect English.

His accent was barely noticeable, Sarah thought to herself. She grabbed his hand and shook it once.

"Hi. It's nice to meet you, Chun-chieh," she said with a smile.

"Please, call me Chun," he said.

He turned his attention back to Susan.

"Before I forget," he said as he leaned down and picked up the roses. "These are for you. There's one for every year I've been in love with you."

Susan placed her hand over her heart. She took the bouquet from Chun-chieh and gently kissed his lips. Her lips released sooner than she wanted them to.

"Thank you. That is so beautiful," she said.

Sarah felt tears form in her eyes. She could not believe what was happening. It was like watching a romantic comedy, she thought. She had never experienced a love so pure and patient as the one she was witnessing unfold in front of her. She suddenly felt out of place. She wanted to give the two of them space, but her flight to Thailand didn't leave until the next day.

"I'm going to go watch the carousel for our luggage," she said.

"I can help," Chun-chieh offered.

"That's OK. I got it. Thank you though," she replied.

Sarah walked toward the carousel and looked back at her aunt and her secret letter lover. He pulled her in close and held her in a way Sarah longed to be held. It was in that moment that she realized why she could never choose between Charlie and Tim. There was something missing with both of them. They both provided her with things the other couldn't. She cared deeply about both of them, but there had to be more out there.

Seeing her aunt with Chun made her decide she wasn't going to settle. Not when it came to love or work or anything. She was going to find her Chun, no matter how long it took. In the meantime, she was going to enjoy her newly acquired single life. She signed and filed the divorce papers the day before they left for their trip. Sixty days after that, she would officially be a divorced woman. But she already felt divorced. She had for a long time.

Her thoughts were discontinued by the sight of their baggage coming near her. She leaned down and picked up her suitcase, followed by Susan's. Her aunt had packed a lot of stuff and Sarah realized she didn't ask her aunt how long she was staying, or if she even planned on returning home. Sarah wouldn't blame her if she decided to stay with Chun. Susan didn't have much in Muncie besides her. Sarah would miss her aunt if she didn't return home, but she would understand. She rolled the two suitcases over toward Chun and Susan.

"I'll take those," Chun said as he grabbed the suitcases from Sarah.

"Thank you," she responded.

Sarah grabbed her carry-on, and she and Susan followed Chun out of the airport to his car. It was a beautiful, sunny day. The temperature was 76-degrees Fahrenheit.

"This weather is gorgeous," Susan observed.

"Autumn is the best time to visit. We're coming off of our rainy season, so the weather is more desirable. Although, it doesn't get too cold here. At least not compared to Indiana. You won't see snow here, unless you climb way up in the mountains," Chun explained. "But I don't recommend that."

Susan laughed.

"The only climbing I'm going to be doing is on top of you," she said.

She immediately blushed. She didn't mean to say that out loud. Sarah's mouth dropped open. She could not believe her aunt just said that. They both looked at Chun to see his reaction. A faint blush was appearing under his tanned skin.

"I would not mind that at all," he responded quietly.

Sarah nudged her aunt in the side playfully. Susan was mortified. She didn't know what to say. There was an awkward silence between the three of them as they continued walking to Chun's car.

"So, besides sex, what's on the agenda today?" Sarah asked jokingly.

Susan glared at her niece, but Sarah was laughing so hard at her own joke she didn't even care. Chun even let out a chuckle, which made Susan feel more at ease.

"Well, I thought you two would be tired after the long flight. So I was going to prepare lunch and then let you two rest. But if you don't want to rest, we could find something to do," he said winking at Susan.

"Rest sounds perfect," Sarah said.

She wasn't tired after sleeping most of the flight, but she was not going to get in the way of her aunt getting laid for what may be the first time in her life. Sarah wondered if her aunt was a virgin. They never talked about that before. Up until a few days ago, they had never talked about Susan's love life in general.

Chun-chieh drove the three of them to his house. He lived in a nice-sized house outside of Taipei in the hills. Most homes in Taiwan are built up instead of out, but Chun had enough land his house expanded both ways. The exterior of the front was covered with giant floor to ceiling windows. Sarah was impressed. She wondered what he did for a living.

They entered the house and Chun gave them a quick tour. Sarah placed her things in one of the guest rooms on the opposite side of the house from Chun's room. She did not want to hear the noises that would be coming from his bedroom that night. After the tour, they sat down in the dining room where he had prepared a feast.

The dining room table was covered with various fruits and vegetables that Chun said were picked fresh that morning. There were also dumplings he claimed were a secret family recipe. Susan wondered if the recipe was his late wife's, but she decided to push Chia-Ling out of her head. She didn't want to think about her. For the main course, Chun served beef noodle soup. He said if you only eat one thing in Taiwan, it has to be beef noodle soup.

Sarah was starving and sampled a little bit of everything. Susan was pickier. She had a small bowl of the soup and a single dumpling. Sarah couldn't tell if her aunt was nervous about what the night might entail or if she was just tired from the flight. Sarah didn't want to ask her in front of Chun. So instead, she thanked Chun for the delicious meal and retreated to her room for the night. She fell asleep dreaming about finding her own secret letter lover.

14

The next morning, Chun and Susan drove Sarah to the airport. Chun stayed in the car while Susan stepped outside to say goodbye to her niece.

"How was last night?" Sarah asked with a wink.

Her aunt immediately blushed and looked her niece in the eyes.

"It was everything I could have ever hoped it would be," she replied sincerely.

Sarah smiled. She was happy her aunt was finally happy.

"There's something I need to tell you," Susan began.

"What's that?" Sarah asked.

"I'm not going back to Muncie. I'm going to stay here with Chun," she answered.

"I figured as much," Sarah said.

She tried to hide the sadness in her voice. She was going to miss her aunt, but she wasn't going to let her leave what she had with Chun behind. Not after all of these years of being a part.

"It's OK. I'll be OK," Sarah said, trying to convince herself more than anything.

Susan grabbed her niece's hands in hers.

"I know you will," she said. "You're a Simmons. It's in our blood. Us Simmons women are strong and resilient. If my relationship with Chun has taught me anything over the years, it is that we can get through anything."

Sarah smiled at her aunt again. She thought back to her own tragedies and didn't know how she survived them. She thought it was because she had Charlie there. He helped her through it all. But maybe she didn't need Charlie. She couldn't need Charlie anymore, she decided. She had to face her tragedies on her own. If her aunt could do it, so could she.

"I love you, Aunt Susan," Sarah said as she wrapped her aunt into a hug.

"I love you too, Sarah," she responded, squeezing Sarah a little too tight.

"Everything is going to be OK," Sarah said, sensing her aunt's reluctance.

"I know it will," Susan replied.

Susan thought about telling her niece about her illness, but she didn't want to damper her trip. Besides, it was all laid out in the letter she left at Sarah's house. She nonchalantly slipped it onto the kitchen table while Sarah was grabbing her luggage the day they left for the airport. Sarah didn't even notice. Now was not the time, she decided as her niece pulled away from the hug. Sarah leaned her head into the passenger window of Chun's car.

"It was nice to meet you, Chun. Take good care of my aunt," she said.

"You know I will," he said with a smile.

That smile almost made Sarah fall in love with him too. She giggled at the thought. Then she remembered Chun had a son. She wondered if he was single and if he was as romantic as his father. Thoughts of the four of them living in Taiwan together flashed through Sarah's head. They diminished as quickly as they had arrived.

She was not going to jump into another relationship so soon, she decided. She was going to Thailand to find herself, no matter how long that took. She needed a break from what had become the normalcy of her life in Muncie. She never wanted to stay in Muncie. The thought of living there her whole life always seemed dreadful to her. But she stayed because of her dad.

He was her home. The only family – besides Aunt Susan – she had ever known. She wasn't going to abandon him. But now that he was gone, and Susan was living in Asia, there wasn't anything holding her down there anymore. She thought about Tim briefly and how their relationship had ended sooner than she would have liked. But he was in love with her and she wasn't sure she felt the same way about him.

He was handsome and checked all of her boxes. But she wondered if there was something more out there for her. She didn't want to work in a bookshop her whole life, she decided. She wanted to do something meaningful, something that would make her want to wake up in the morning. She didn't know what that was, but she hoped to find it in Thailand.

She gave her aunt one more quick hug and then wheeled her luggage inside the airport. She checked her bag, went through security, and then sat at a little café near her gate. She once again found herself looking around at all the other travelers. They were all lost in their own world, completely oblivious to their surroundings. She wondered if that had been her on previous expeditions. She realized it had.

She sipped on her coffee and continued people watching. Her eyes caught the eyes of a young, attractive man who appeared to be about her age. She continued looking at him as he stared at her. He looked familiar, but she couldn't place his face. Suddenly, he stood up and walked toward her.

"Excuse me, miss. Can I sit here?" he asked as he pointed to the empty chair next to her.

He had an Italian accent. Sarah suddenly remembered his face.

"Luca?" she asked with a wide-eyed grin.

He smiled as he took a seat.

"I thought you looked familiar, but I didn't know if you would remember me. Our time together was so brief," he said. "Sarah, correct?"

"Yes. Oh my gosh. How are you? What are you doing in Taiwan?" she asked.

She had so many questions. She was also impressed at how small the world really is. Luca was more attractive than she remembered. She never thought she was going to see him again after she abandoned him on their date in Italy nearly six months prior. She also couldn't believe it had only been six months. She felt like she had lived a lifetime since then.

"I am doing well. I'm holidaying in Asia for a bit. I started here. Now I'm heading to Thailand and then the Maldives after that. I wanted to experience some beaches other than Italy's. What are you doing here?" he asked.

Sarah didn't hear what he said after he mentioned going to Thailand. She wasn't a religious person and didn't believe in signs, but she definitely thought this was a sign. She noticed he had stopped talking and was looking at her to answer.

"I'm sorry. What did you say?" she asked.

He let out a laugh.

"I asked what you're doing here," he said.

"It's a long story involving a secret love affair with my aunt. But now I'm heading to Thailand as well," she said with a grin.

"Are you traveling with anyone?" he asked looking around. "A boyfriend perhaps?"

She chuckled at his sly attempt to find out if she was still single.

"No. I'm traveling solo," she said.

"Well, would you look at that. I am also traveling alone," he replied with a smirk.

"So, what are you going to do in Thailand?" she asked.

"I'm not quite sure. I'm letting this trip take me where it takes me. But I want to spend a few days in Phuket for sure," he replied. "What about you?"

"I'm pretty much doing the same. I have my first three nights booked in Bangkok, but after that it's an open book. But I wanted to visit Phuket as well," she answered with a smile.

"Well, it sounds like this trip might take me to Bangkok for a few days," he said. "I mean, that is if you don't mind having a familiar face around. If you would rather travel by yourself, I completely understand. But you still owe me that date."

Sarah laughed. She was looking forward to traveling by herself, but it was nice to see Luca again.

And he looked good. Really good. She pictured the two of them exploring Thailand together – climbing mountains, frolicking together on the beach. A few days with him wouldn't hurt, she decided.

"Oh, I owe you, do I?" she asked playfully.

"You sure do," he answered.

"What did you have in mind?" she asked.

Their conversation was interrupted by the boarding announcement. They both stood up and took their place in line to board the plane. After boarding, Sarah convinced one of the flight attendants to let her switch her seat to the open seat next to Luca.

"Hi. I hope you don't mind, but the flight attendant said I could sit here," she said as she sat next to him.

"Not at all," Luca replied.

"So, about that date," Sarah said.

"We don't have to go on a date. I was just joking around," he replied.

"Oh," she said sadly.

"I mean, unless you want to. I could try to squeeze you into my schedule," he said arrogantly.

Sarah wasn't the type of woman who liked arrogant men. They usually turned her off. But there was something about Luca that intrigued her. He was playing hard to get and Sarah was up for the challenge.

"That's OK. Bangkok is a big city and there's plenty of things to do to keep me busy," she said.

"I'm sure there is. But it won't be as satisfying," he said confidently.

Sarah looked at him. She was trying to read his face. She could tell he was flirting with her, but she couldn't tell if he was being serious or if this was just a game for him.

"I could say the same thing to you," she said coyly.

"Alright then. How about we exchange phone numbers and we'll figure something out?" he asked.

"That works for me," she said.

"Good. Now tell me about this secret love affair. I'm intrigued," he said after they exchanged numbers.

Sarah laughed and began telling him the story about Susan and Chun. Even though it was still new to her, and Luca was the first person she was telling, it had become her favorite story. She told the story with such enthusiasm it was like she was reading a fairytale. She mentioned all of the details, including the dozens of roses – *one for every year I've been in love with you.*

"That is truly beautiful," Luca said when she finished.

"I know. I still can't believe she kept it a secret this whole time," she replied.

"Yeah. That's something else. But I get it," he said.

"You do?" Sarah asked.

"Yeah. It seemed so perfect on paper. She was worried if she told someone, their judgement or reaction would tamper with her feelings. She didn't want anything to ruin what she had, even if it was only through letters. I probably would have done the same thing," he answered.

"You would have stayed in a relationship that was based solely on letter writing without any physical contact for decades?" she asked questioningly.

"Oh no. I would definitely be having physical relationships. But the letter writing, I could keep that a secret," he said.

She didn't know how to respond so she shifted her gaze out the window. Luca thought his comment made her uncomfortable, so he changed the topic.

"What do you plan to do in Bangkok?" he asked.

She returned her gaze back to his face. His skin appeared smooth and he had a perfectly trimmed beard and mustache. That was one of Sarah's weaknesses. She loved a man with a beard. Although, neither Charlie nor Tim had beards. She got lost in his beauty and had forgotten what he asked her.

"I'm sorry, what did you ask?" she asked.

Luca chuckled. He liked when Sarah lost her train of thought.

"What do you plan to do in Bangkok?" he asked again.

You, she thought to herself.

"I don't really have any plans. I'm open for anything," she said suggestively.

"Is that so?" Luca asked with a wink.

Sarah giggled and nodded her head.

"I think we're going to have a fun adventure, Miss Sarah," he said.

"I think so too, Mr. Luca," she responded playfully.

He reached his hand over and grabbed Sarah's hand. She smiled at him. She barely knew this man, but she was already comfortable with him. She pushed the armrest up that was between them and leaned back against his chest. He wrapped one arm around her and rested it on her waist, while the other remained holding her hand.

The two of them fell asleep like that. Luca was the first one to wake up. He looked down and saw Sarah was still sound asleep. He leaned down and kissed her lightly on the forehead. Her lips curled up into a smile and she slowly opened her eyes. She looked up at him.

"Good morning," he said with a smile.

Then he looked at his watch.

"Or afternoon I guess," he said with a laugh.

Sarah giggled and pulled his arm so it was around her stomach. She held it there and adjusted her head on his chest so it was easier to see him.

"How long until we land?" she asked.

He looked at his watch again.

"Probably another hour or so," he said. "You can go back to sleep if you'd like. I promise I won't wake you again."

She smiled at him.

"That's OK," she replied. "I'm content just like this."

"Good," he said as he wrapped his other arm around her. "Tell me something about yourself, Sarah."

"What would you like to know?" she asked.

"Everything," he answered.

She laughed.

"We don't have time for everything," she said.

"OK. Then what have you been up to since we last saw each other?" he asked.

Sarah didn't know how to answer that question. A lot had happened in her life. If she divulged all of that information to Luca right now, it might scare him away, she thought. Especially the part of her getting married and divorced so soon, she added.

"Next question," she said with a smile.

Luca laughed.

"C'mon. It can't be that bad," he said.

She gave him a serious look.

"It was the worst six months of my life," she responded sadly.

He tightened his grip around her.

"I'm so sorry to hear that. We don't have to talk about it," he said.

He leaned his head down and kissed her forehead again. She smiled up at him.

"Thank you," she said. "How about you tell me something about yourself?"

"What would you like to know?" he asked.

"How are you single?" she asked.

"Who said I was single?" he replied jokingly.

Sarah went to sit up, but Luca held her against him.

"I'm kidding. I'm single because I choose to be. I haven't met the girl that I want to change this lifestyle for," he replied.

Sarah wondered how many girls Luca has had sex with. He really enjoyed being single, she thought. Then she thought about her number and realized it was up there. She enjoyed sex, and the number of partners one person has had doesn't define them as a person, she decided.

"That makes sense," she said.

"Why are you single?" he asked. "Surely, you have lots of guys doting over you."

"I wouldn't say lots," she said laughing. "There are, or there were, two guys back home. I'm in the process of divorcing the one and as for the other, well, I'm here now."

"Wait. You're married?" Luca asked.

"It's a long story," Sarah replied.

"But you weren't married when we met, correct?" he asked.

"Correct," she answered.

"I see," he said confused. "I guess a lot has happened since the spring."

"You have no idea," she replied.

He gave her a light squeeze.

"All that matters is we're both here now," he said with a devilish grin.

Sarah smiled. She liked the sound of that. And she liked the idea of exploring a foreign country with a sexy Italian man even more.

"I agree," she said.

She leaned her head up and kissed Luca right on the lips. He was taken aback, but he kissed her back. Sarah turned her body to face him and kissed him again. This time a little bit harder. Then she remembered they were on a plane, surrounded by other people. She quickly pulled away and blushed.

"Maybe we should save that for the hostel," she said with a wink.

"A hostel?" Luca asked, almost disgusted.

"That's where I'm staying," Sarah replied.

"Oh no, no, no. I will get us a hotel room. That is, if you're comfortable sharing a room with me," he said.

Sarah barely knew this man. She didn't even know his last name. All she really knew about him was he was from Italy. She knew this could potentially be dangerous, but she didn't care. All she wanted was to rip his clothes off and spend the entire day making love to him.

"I'm in," she said excitedly.

15

Luca rented them a hotel room in the Bangkok Riverside district for two nights. After that, they would decide if they wanted to continue traveling together or go their separate ways. The hotel room was quaint. There was a queen-sized bed that took up most of the room, and directly in front of it was a small entertainment center with a 43-inch flatscreen TV. A small closet sat at the end of a narrow hallway that led to the bathroom. The bathroom was small with a single vanity sink, a toilet, and a shower. It reminded Sarah of a cruise ship bathroom.

But it beat staying in a hostel and sharing a bathroom with strangers, she decided. Besides, they really only needed a bed, she thought. She pushed her luggage under the bed so it wouldn't take up what little space they had. Luca did the same.

"What would you like to do first?" she asked as she turned to face him.

Luca smiled at her and gently pushed her back onto the bed. He climbed on top of her and pressed his lips against hers. He kissed her softly at first and then more aggressively. He slipped his tongue into her mouth and then back into his. He grabbed her shirt and lifted it over her head, tossing it on the ground.

He admired her small, yet perky breasts as they peeked out of her purple-laced bra. He sat up, bringing her with him, and gently traced his fingers across the lace. He reached around her back and unclasped her bra. He gently pulled the straps down her arms and tossed the bra onto her shirt.

He leaned down and lightly kissed the top of her breast before moving his way down to her nipple. He placed it in his mouth and gave it a light suck. Sarah tilted her head back and let out a soft moan. Luca pushed her onto her back and unbuttoned her jeans. He pulled them off in a hurry and stared at her as she laid on the bed wearing nothing but a thin pair of panties.

He stared at her as if he were about to devour her. The look in his eyes excited Sarah. She couldn't remember the last time a man looked at her that way. She could feel her wetness seeping through her panties. She was ready.

Luca stood before her and slowly removed his shirt, revealing a chiseled chest and stomach. His muscles weren't as bulky as Charlie's, but they were very much defined. He smiled at Sarah's pleased reaction to his body. He moved his hands to his belt and quickly removed it, tossing it to the floor. Then he pulled his pants down and slowly stepped out of them. He stood in front of Sarah in his black boxer briefs letting her admire the view before he made his way on top of her.

He climbed up her body until his face was inches away from hers. He gave her a devilish grin before kissing her hard on the mouth. He moved his right hand up her body and grabbed her breast, giving it a squeeze. Her breathing accelerated as Luca moved his lips to her neck. He pulled a small patch of skin into his mouth with his lips and gave it a light suck. Sarah let out a soft moan.

Luca rolled to the side of her and traced his hand down her stomach. He slipped it under her panties and down to her vagina. He rubbed her clit back and forth a few times before continuing south. Sarah arched her back and let out another moan. She was impatient and wanted him inside of her already, but Tim showed her it is worth the wait.

She didn't want to think about Tim in that moment. She wanted to think about Luca. Just then, he thrusted one finger inside of her. She began to breathe harder and the thought of Tim was gone. He moved his finger in and out a few times before he thrusted another finger inside of her.

She arched her back again. She never noticed his hands before, but his fingers were thick, she realized. She could feel them on both sides of her vaginal wall. He continued to move them harder and faster. She could hear them sliding against her wetness. She couldn't take it anymore.

"I want you," she called out.

He grinned at her and removed his fingers. He moved his hand out from her underwear and quickly pulled her panties down her leg, tossing them onto the floor. He was about to make his way on top of Sarah, but she rolled him onto his back and climbed on top of him. She kissed her way down his body in a hurry and pulled down his boxer briefs.

She was slightly taken aback by his uncircumcised penis, but then she remembered most Europeans weren't circumcised. To her surprise, he was already erect. She pulled the extra skin down to reveal the head and shaft. Then she lowered her mouth on top of the head and pushed his penis to the back of her throat. She moved her mouth up and down while swirling her tongue around the sides of his penis. Luca moaned loudly. She added her hand to the mix and moved it in a synchronized motion with her mouth.

"I need you," Luca said slightly louder than a whisper.

Sarah released his penis from the grips of her mouth and smiled up at him. He pulled her up toward him and rolled her onto her back. He jumped off the bed and ran to his backpack. He fumbled around inside before pulling out a condom. He ripped it open and slid it onto his penis. Then he climbed back onto the bed and over Sarah.

He guided his manhood into her vagina slowly. She moaned as she felt the head enter. Then she moaned louder as she surrounded his entire shaft. He held her hip with one hand and held himself up with the other as he thrusted into her. He moved in and out slowly. Then he continued to move harder and faster. She wanted to call out his name, but she couldn't form the word. She was surrounded in pleasure.

Her whole body tensed up, then she felt a sensational release. Just then, Luca collapsed on top of her. She wrapped her arms around him and held him there. She felt the most relaxed she had felt in a long time, as if all of her worries were just fucked away. She didn't want that moment to end. She wanted to lay there naked with Luca for the rest of eternity.

After a moment of the two of them catching their breath, Luca lifted his head up and kissed her lightly on the lips. She smiled at him.

"That was incredible," he said.

"It really was," she replied.

"I don't want to move," he said as he laid his head back down on her chest.

"Don't," she said.

"I should probably get cleaned up though," he said.

"OK. But then come right back," she said.

"You don't have to worry about that. I'm not going anywhere," he said before kissing her again.

He slowly climbed off of the bed and walked down the narrow hallway to the bathroom. Sarah laid in bed with a smile plastered across her face. She heard the shower turn on. She pictured the two of them having shower sex, but that wouldn't happen here. The shower was too small. Maybe their next stop, if they had a next stop, she thought.

She pictured the two of them fucking their way across Thailand. That wouldn't be a productive way to see all of the different sights, but it would be fun, she thought. Afterall, they were in the Land of Smiles. She rolled over on her side to face the only window in the room. It looked out over the Chao Phraya River. It was getting dark out and she realized they had not eaten dinner. Her stomach rumbled.

The shower turned off. A few moments later, Luca appeared wearing nothing but a towel. Sarah noticed how his hips swayed ever so lightly when he walked. Then the towel fell to the ground, revealing his shriveled up, uncircumcised penis. She wanted to laugh at the sight of it, but she knew better. Instead, she smiled up at him.

"What would you like to do now?" he asked as he climbed back into bed.

He pressed his naked body against Sarah's and draped an arm across her chest. His hand rested on the side of her breast. She turned her head toward him.

"Do you think we could get some food delivered?" she asked.

"I think we can get whatever you want," he said as he pressed his lips against hers.

She smiled.

"I would like Thai food," she suggested.

"I don't think that will be hard to find," he laughed.

He climbed to the end of the bed and pulled his cell phone out of his pants pocket. He returned to his position next to Sarah and began searching the internet for restaurants that delivered to their hotel. There were more options than he expected.

"There's essentially everything. Are you sure you want Thai?" he asked.

"Yes, please," she replied.

"OK. What would you like?" he asked.

"Surprise me," she replied.

"Do you want chicken, pork, beef, seafood?" he asked.

"Surprise me. Except no seafood," she replied.

"OK. Negative on the seafood," he noted.

He called one of the restaurants and ordered three entrees (chicken, pork, and beef), fried rice, fried noodles, and an order of thot man khao phot – a deep-fried corn fritter with various Thai ingredients.

"There's no way we're going to be able to eat all of that," Sarah said after Luca got off of the phone.

"I know, but I wanted to make sure you had something you liked," he replied.

"I would have been fine with one entrée. I don't need three," she laughed.

"Well, now I know for next time," he replied with a smile. "It will be here in about 20 minutes."

"That's quick," she said.

"But it still gives us time if you want to do that again," he said suggestively.

"You're ready to go again?" she asked.

He laughed at the shocked tone in her voice.

"Us Italians are always ready," he said jokingly.

"Good to know," she said as she started to make her way on top of him.

But he pushed her down onto her back and climbed on top of her. He quickly made his way down to her vagina and gently kissed her clitoris. The sensual feeling of his lips against her sent a chill up her spine. He swiped his tongue down the inside of the lips and lightly flicked it against her opening. She let out a soft moan.

He thrusted his tongue inside her and flicked it up and down. Sarah moaned louder. He pushed his tongue further inside her. She continued to moan. Her heart was pounding so hard she could feel her pulse in her face.

"Fuck me," she called out.

Luca didn't need to be asked twice. He quickly removed his tongue and rushed to his backpack. His box of condoms was already open and on top. He grabbed one out of the box and slid it onto his already-erect penis. He went to make his way on top of Sarah, but she rolled him over and climbed on top of him.

She grabbed his manhood with one hand and positioned it below her vagina. She slowly slid down it like a fireman's pole. Luca's breathing accelerated. She slid down until he was all the way inside her. She rocked her hips back and forth over him, pushing harder and harder into him. They moaned together.

She was about to move faster, but Luca rolled her over onto her back. He held her shoulder with one hand and the headboard with his other. He thrusted into her as hard as he could. She called out his name.

"I love that," he said in-between breaths.

He continued to thrust into her hard and fast. She called out his name again. Her back arched and she felt a release. Luca thrusted two more times before he collapsed on top of her. They both laid there out of breath, unable to move.

Then there was a knock on their door. Their food had arrived. Luca quickly jumped out of bed and put his pants on, with the now-used condom hanging loosely from his penis. He forgot his underwear. He opened the door shirtless.

"Hello," a young Thai man said. "The total is 425 baht."

"Here you go. You can keep the change," Luca said, handing him 500 baht. "Thank you."

"Thank you so much, sir," the delivery man said as he handed the food to Luca.

"You're welcome. Have a good night," he replied.

He closed the door and placed the food on the entertainment center. Then he removed his pants. Sarah laughed.

"What? You're still naked. So I should be naked too," he responded.

"That makes sense," she replied.

"I'm going to go take care of this quick though," he said, pointing to the condom.

Sarah laughed again.

"Sounds good," she said.

He went to the bathroom and returned a few moments later.

"What would you like to eat first?" he asked.

"All of it," she answered.

"Perfect," he said.

He grabbed the food and placed the separate containers at the foot of the bed. Sarah scooted to the food and picked up a thot man khao phot with her fingers. She took a small bite to taste it.

"That is delicious," she said.

"Really?" Luca asked surprised.

"Mhm. Try it," she said as she held it out to him.

He leaned forward and placed his lips around it, breaking off a piece in his mouth. He gently chewed it and smiled.

"That is delicious," he said.

"I told you," she said smiling.

They both sampled a little bit of everything until they were too full to move. It was all delicious, they agreed. They laid on their backs holding their stomachs.

"I ate too much," Sarah said.

"Me too," Luca replied.

She turned her head toward him.

"Have I ever told you how absolutely beautiful you are?" she asked.

Luca laughed.

"You're not too bad yourself," he replied.

"I'm sure my hair is a mess. I don't have makeup on. And I am bloated from eating too much," she replied.

He gently caressed the side of her face.

"You don't need makeup. You are beautiful without it," he said.

She smiled. When his arrogance wasn't showing, he was really sweet, she thought. She didn't notice that before. Although, their time together in Italy was fleeting. She didn't know how to respond so she didn't say anything. Luca sat up and began cleaning up their dinner.

"I can help," Sarah said as she sat up.

"It's OK. I can do it. You just lay there," he said as he smiled at her naked body.

She suddenly became aware of her nakedness and covered her breasts with her arms. Then she removed her arms. He had already seen her naked and experienced her body, she thought.

Meanwhile, Luca threw away what was left of their food. He turned to face her.

"We should probably try to get some sleep. We have a big day tomorrow," he said.

Sarah looked at him quizzically.

"What's tomorrow?" she asked.

"Well, we're going to do that again," he said motioning toward the bed. "A lot."

She laughed.

"Deal," she said.

"And we have to go see the sights," he added.

"What do you want to see?" she asked.

"Everything. But mostly you," he said as he climbed back into bed and kissed her on the lips.

She kissed him back.

"I like the sound of that," she said.

The two of them climbed under the covers, their naked bodies touching. Luca held her in his arms until they both fell asleep.

16

Sarah and Luca spent the day touring Bangkok's must-see places. They climbed Wat Arun and were in awe at the view of the Chao Phraya River. At the top of the tower, Luca grabbed Sarah in his arms and dipped her. He gave her the most passionate kiss she had ever received. Once he stood her back up, she was completely speechless. She just blushed and smiled at him.

She wasn't a big fan of public displays of affection, but no one was paying any attention to them. They were surrounded by other tourists too engaged with the view. Sarah was too busy replaying that kiss in her head to realize Luca was talking to her.

"You went away again," he said laughing.

She finally realized he was talking to her.

"I'm sorry," she laughed. "What did you say?"

"I asked if you were ready to move on," he replied.

"Oh, yes. Where to next?" she asked.

"It's a surprise," he said, grabbing her hand.

Holding hands, he led her back down the narrow stairs of the temple and onto the busy, crowded streets of Bangkok. He held her close so he wouldn't lose her in the crowd, and he liked the feeling of her body next to his. He led her down to a dock by the river where they jumped aboard the public river boat. They got off at Pier 5 and headed to Chinatown.

They got takeaway from a Thai-Chinese street food vendor and sat on a rickety, old wooden bench to eat. Sarah marveled at the narrow streets and how the drivers managed to squeeze around each other without crashing. She was used to narrow streets and smaller vehicles from her trips to Europe, but it was different in Asia. Everything was more compact and there were a lot more people.

Once they finished their lunch, they stopped at a small shop where an elderly woman was selling hand-painted pottery. Sarah bought a small pot that was painted blue and white. She planned to plant a succulent in it once she returned home to Muncie. After that, they went back to the pier and boarded the river boat again. This time, they got off at the stop for the Grand Palace.

They strolled through the different complexes at the palace for a few hours. They were both amazed at the condition and colors of the walls. Sarah had explored several palaces in her journeys, but the Grand Palace was something else. She especially loved the Emerald Buddha.

By the time they exited the palace, the sexual tension between them was hotter than the 90-degree day it was turning out to be. Luca pinned Sarah up against one of the white columns and kissed her like he did at the top of Wat Arun. Her heart began to beat faster. She wanted him to rip her clothes off and take her right there, but she knew that wasn't an option. She pulled her lips away from his.

"Let's go back to the hotel," she whispered in his ear.

He pulled away with a childish grin. He grabbed her hand and the two of them ran the whole way back to the river boat, practically bumping into several people along the way. They yelled out meaningless apologies. They were both too horny to care. They got off at the pier near their hotel. The walk from the pier to their room was a blur.

The next thing Sarah knew, they were inside the room undressing each other in record fashion. She knew she was already wet and ready to go. Luca must have been ready too because as soon as the last piece of clothing had been removed, he swept her up in his arms and laid her on the bed. He didn't bother with a condom this time, he just entered her. Sarah wanted to protest because she wasn't on birth control anymore, but the feeling of his skin against her felt too good.

"We need to be careful," she called out in-between breaths.

"I will. I promise," he replied.

He leaned down into her and kissed her neck. She let out a soft sigh. Then he thrusted into her as hard as he could, and she screamed out in pleasure. He gripped the edge of the mattress for support and continued thrusting into her hard. She moaned again. She didn't want the feeling to end. But then, Luca quickly pulled himself out of her and ran to the bathroom.

Growing Love

She was left lying there not fully satisfied. She heard the shower turn on and imagined it would be a few minutes before he returned. She ventured her fingers down between her legs and pushed two of them inside. She closed her mouth to stifle her moan. She moved her fingers in and out, harder and faster. She was too caught up in her own pleasure to notice the shower had turned off and Luca had returned to the bedroom.

"Oh my God," he said as he stared at her.

Sarah immediately became embarrassed and pulled her fingers out. Her face showed panic. She didn't know what to say.

"No, keep going. That is so fucking sexy," he replied.

She let out a nervous laugh.

"What?" she asked.

"I've never seen a girl do that before. But oh my God is that sexy. I love that you can pleasure yourself. I'm sorry I wasn't able to this time," he said.

"Well, you can still come here and get the job done," she said with a smirk.

She didn't know where this newfound sense of confidence came from, but she suddenly felt very empowered. Luca made his way back onto the bed and kissed her lightly on the lips.

"What would you like me to do, my lady?" he asked.

"Your fingers will suffice, sir," she replied with a giggle.

He rolled to her side and tip-toed his fingers down her body until he reached her vagina. He gently rubbed her clitoris with his index finger, causing her to bite down on her lower lip. He continued south until he reached her opening. Then he slowly inserted his index finger. He moved it in and out a few times before it was joined by his middle finger. She had forgotten about the girth of his fingers until they were inside her again.

He thrusted his two fingers as far as he could, and Sarah let out a moan. He pulled them about halfway out and pushed them into her as hard as he could. She moaned again. He continued doing that until Sarah arched her back and he could feel her release. He slowly pulled his fingers out and wiped the wetness on the inside of her thigh.

"Now I think it's your turn to go get cleaned up," he said smiling at her.

"Come here," she said, pulling his face toward hers.

She kissed him hard on the mouth, sliding her tongue into his. He made his way on top of her, kissing her back. She could feel his penis growing hard against her skin. She pulled away from the kiss and looked at him quizzically.

"Like I said, us Italians are always ready," he said laughing.

"OK," she said.

"Really?" he asked with a grin.

"Sure. I can go again," she said, returning his smile.

"Oh my God. I think I love you Sarah," he said jokingly.

"Don't say that," she laughed.

She knew it was said as a joke, but she didn't want to think about love. She had spent the last few months thinking about love. Did she love Charlie? Did she love Tim? Maybe she didn't love either of them, she decided. Maybe she had never been in love, she thought. What even is love, she asked herself.

Her philosophical thoughts were interrupted by the feeling of Luca's breath on her vagina. She didn't even notice he had made his way down there. Then his tongue was inside her and she was transported to a world of pleasure. All of her concerns about love, or lack of love, disappeared. Luca was the distraction she had needed.

After their second round of lovemaking, they both laid there out of breath for several minutes. Then slowly, Luca climbed off the bed and pulled Sarah's hand toward him.

"Come on," he said.

"Where are we going?" she asked.

"To shower," he replied.

"We both can't fit in there," she laughed.

"We'll make it work," he replied.

He led her by the hand to the tiny bathroom. He turned the shower on and adjusted the temperature until the water was a comfortable warmth. He let Sarah step inside before he slid in behind her. Their bodies were touching in the small confines of the shower.

"This isn't going to work," she laughed.

"Of course it will. When you need to turn, I'll turn with you," he replied. "Besides, isn't this nice?"

He turned Sarah around so she was facing him. He lifted her chin up and kissed her lightly on the lips. Water poured down over their faces and down their naked bodies.

"It is," she agreed.

She pushed him against the wall of the shower and kissed him again, forcing her tongue into his mouth.

His hands were drawn to her body like it was clay and he was her sculptor. He moved them slowly over his masterpiece, memorizing every curve and every line. When he reached her ass, he grabbed it firmly.

Sarah pulled her lips away from his and let out a light moan. She liked being handled like that. She didn't like being treated like a delicate flower.

"Fuck me," she said.

"Right now?" he asked surprised.

"Yes," she answered.

"How?" he asked.

"I don't know. Just do it," she said more demanding than she meant to.

Luca picked Sarah up and she wrapped her legs around his waist. He turned them around so her back was pinned against the wall. He looked at her with a question in his eyes. She nodded her head yes. He leaned his head towards her and kissed her hard on the mouth. Then he entered her aggressively. She pulled her head back and leaned it against the wall.

"Yes," she cried out.

He slammed into her harder and harder as water continued to rain down on them. She was screaming with pleasure.

"Don't stop," she pleaded.

Luca was exhausted, but he wanted to please her. So he pushed past the exhaustion and kept going. Finally, Sarah let out a final moan and her body relaxed into him. He extracted himself from the depths of her vagina and slowly placed her feet back on the ground. Her legs trembled slightly, and she held onto him for support.

"That was amazing," she said.

She looked down at his still-erect penis.

"You didn't finish," she noted.

"I don't think I can," he said. "I need time to reload."

She smiled and gave him a light kiss on the lips.

"Thank you for that," she said.

"Any time," he replied, kissing her back.

They finished their shower and dried off with the tiny towels that were supplied in the bathroom. Then they both collapsed on the bed naked. Sarah rolled onto her side to face him.

"I could do that all day," she said

"You're going to kill me, aren't you?" he asked laughing.

"There are worse ways to die," she replied with a wink.

"That's true," he said.

He lifted his head up, gave her a light kiss on the lips, and laid back down.

"Besides, I thought Italians were always ready," she joked.

"That was before I knew Americans were such sexual creatures," he replied.

"They're not. I'm an oddity," she said smiling.

"I like you, Sarah," he said seriously.

"I like you too, Luca," she replied.

But those words scared her. She didn't want to start another relationship so soon. She came to Thailand to find herself – whatever that meant. She knew she allowed herself to be distracted by Luca, but she thought it would be a few day fling and they would go on their way. But after being with him, she realized she could spend her whole trip in bed with him. He satisfied her in a way only Tim had. Tim.

She thought about the sexy nurse waiting for her back in Muncie. She saw him the night before she and Susan left. It was the first time she saw him since she told Charlie she was leaving him. To her surprise, he encouraged her to go to Thailand. He said it would be good for her. He probably never imagined she would be spending the trip in bed with another man, she thought. Suddenly she felt guilty.

She wasn't technically doing anything wrong. She hadn't officially gotten back together with Tim. It was just implied that it was going to happen, she thought. But she knew he would not be happy if he knew what she was doing. She was lost in her own thoughts she didn't realize Luca was talking to her. His laughter brought her back to the present.

"What's so funny?" she asked confused.

"You disappeared again," he said.

"Oh," she said embarrassed.

"No, it's cute," he replied.

"What were you saying?" she asked.

"I was asking you what you would like to eat for dinner. We can go somewhere or get something delivered again," he said.

"What are our options for delivery?" she asked.

"Whatever your heart desires," he replied.

She knew he was talking about food, but Sarah didn't know what her heart desired. Was it him? Was it Tim? She felt more confused now than she did at the start of the trip.

"You can pick this time. I like anything except seafood," she said.

"Are you sure?" he asked.

"Positive," she replied.

"How about Indian food?" he asked.

Sarah had never had Indian food before. There was only one Indian restaurant in Muncie, and she had never been there.

"Sure," she said.

"What would you like?" he asked.

"I've never had Indian food before. So order us something good. I trust you," she said.

"You shouldn't," he said with a devilish grin. "But you've never had Indian food before?"

"Nope," she replied.

"What kind of sheltered life have you been living?" he asked.

She laughed.

Luca stole a kiss from her before placing the order. He ordered two different entrees, one lamb and one chicken. He also ordered samosas for an appetizer. About 15 minutes later, the food arrived. Luca quickly put on some pants and answered the door. He paid the delivery man and placed the food at the foot of the bed. Then he removed his pants and joined Sarah at the end of the bed.

They immediately began devouring the food. Sarah was impressed at the intensity of the flavors in both dishes. All of the different spices filled her mouth, leaving her wanting more.

"This is delicious," she remarked.

"Good. I'm glad you like it," he replied.

This time, there weren't any leftovers. They had worked up an appetite where they ate every last bite. Luca threw away the empty containers and climbed back into bed with Sarah. The exhaustion of the day was weighing down on both of them. It wasn't long before they fell asleep.

17

The next morning, they had to check out of their hotel. They hadn't discussed if they would continue traveling together or go their separate ways. Sarah was torn about the decision. She knew she wouldn't accomplish what she went to Thailand for if she stayed with Luca, but she enjoyed having him around. It was nice having someone to explore with and then make passionate love to at the end of the day.

He was a good travel companion. He was knowledgeable about the culture and had great taste when it came to food. As for the bedroom aspect, he was a very giving lover. Sarah knew she was making him exhausted, but she could not get enough of him. Especially when he spoke. She was a sucker for European accents.

As they finished packing up the last of their belongings, they turned to look at each other. They knew the time had come to discuss the next step. Neither of them wanted to say goodbye. Nor did they want to seem eager to stay together in case the other one wanted to continue traveling solo. Afterall, that is what they both went to Thailand to do. It was a moment of chance they ended up in the same place at the same time. Someone more naïve might even say it was destiny.

Luca dropped his luggage to the floor and Sarah ran into his arms. Their lips met, igniting a fire inside them. They threw each other's clothes off and Luca was inside of her within minutes. He grunted as he thrusted into her. She called out his name.

"Say it again," he demanded.

"Luca," she called out again.

He continued pushing into her harder and harder. Sarah let out a pleasurable cry as she reached climax. Shortly after, he quickly pulled out and released himself onto her stomach. He looked at her with flushed cheeks, but she didn't seem to mind.

"One last shower?" she asked.

He nodded his head and led her to the shower. They quickly rinsed off in the confined space and then used the towels to dry off. While they were getting dressed, Luca grabbed Sarah's hands.

"Come to Phuket with me," he said.

She looked into his eyes and could see the longing in them. She had planned to go to Phuket after Bangkok, so it wouldn't be derailing her plans, she decided. But she knew she came to Thailand for a reason, and she couldn't find that reason between the sheets with a sexy foreign man. Or could she, she thought.

"OK," she said with a smile.

"Really?" he asked excitedly.

"Yes," she replied.

He picked her up in his arms and swung her around in a circle. When he placed her back on the ground, he held her face in his hands and gave her a long, slow kiss. When he pulled away, he stared into her eyes.

"We're going to have so much fun," he said with a grin.

"I know we will," she replied.

"Have you ever had sex on a beach?" he asked.

She put her finger to her chin and tried to think back on all her sexual encounters.

"I don't think so," she answered.

"Oh good. I'll be your first," he said with a wink.

"I can't wait," she said laughing.

"And I'm also probably your first Italian," he said.

"Mm. Not quite," she replied.

"What?" he asked.

She shrugged.

"OK. I'm at least the best Italian," he suggested.

"OK. We can go with that," she laughed.

He smiled.

"Good," he said.

Four hours later, their plane had landed in Phuket. As soon as the wheels hit the runway, Luca changed into a different person. Sarah sensed he was becoming possessive of her, which she didn't like. But she convinced herself she was reading too much into his change in attitude. He forcefully grabbed her hand as they waited for the plane to pull up to the passenger boarding bridge. She looked at him and saw something in his eyes she didn't notice before. They seemed darker and full of danger. The hairs on the back of her neck stood up.

Then he turned toward her and smiled. His eyes softened, and her neck hairs laid back down. He seemed to be unequivocally happy. She envied him. She wished she could feel that way. She was happy in that moment, excited even, but the guilt of being there with Luca while Tim was back in Muncie crept in the back of her mind. She tried to ignore those thoughts and be focused on the present, but it was hard. It should be Tim next to her on that plane, she decided.

"Is everything OK?" Luca asked.

"Yeah. I think I'm just tired," she lied.

"Did I wear you out?" he joked.

"Something like that," she said giggling.

"When we get to the hotel, you can take a nap by the pool," he said.

"You already booked a room?" she asked.

"I booked this room, well technically it's a villa, when I first started planning this trip. It's the main reason I came to Thailand. Now it's a bonus that I get to share it with you," he said.

"We're staying in a villa?" she asked shockingly.

"Yes, signora. And we have our own private infinity pool. But the hotel is on Kata Noi Beach, so we can go there as well," he said.

"Our own private pool?" she asked.

"Yes," Luca replied.

Sarah couldn't believe it. She knew the euro and the U.S. dollar were both worth significantly more than the baht, but a villa still had to be expensive. She realized she didn't know what Luca did for a living. She wondered if he was in the mafia. She eyed his physique and decided he didn't look like a mobster.

"What?" he asked.

"I'm just surprised," she replied.

"You've never gone somewhere for a specific hotel?" he asked.

"No. I go for the sights and usually stay in hostels," Sarah replied.

"Oh, no signora. You will not be sleeping in any hostels when you're with me," he said while laughing.

He lifted her hand to his lips and gently kissed the back of it.

"You're too beautiful for that. You deserve to experience the finer things in life. Starting with this villa," he said excitedly.

Sarah wanted to ask him what he did for work, but she felt embarrassed they had spent all of this time together and she didn't know. Then she realized she didn't know anything about him besides his name, and what he looked like naked. She hadn't bothered to ask him anything about his personal life. Then she realized he didn't bother asking her anything either. They didn't know each other.

Her thoughts were interrupted by the pilot's announcement they had landed and were cleared to exit the plane. She followed Luca off the plane and to the baggage claim area where they waited for their luggage. Standing there, she couldn't help but think about Tim. She knew so much about him – his favorite color, where he grew up, his favorite food, the way his eyes twinkled when he was genuinely happy, and the way they were glossy when he was sad. She was too consumed in missing Tim she didn't realize Luca had been talking to her.

"You're doing it again," he said.

He sounded annoyed this time.

"What?" she asked.

"You disappeared again," he said.

"I'm sorry. I'm just tired," she lied.

"Are you sure? You seem like you have a lot going on," he said.

"I just need a nap and then I'll be good to go," she said, forcing a smile.

"OK, good. Because you're going to love this place," he said.

"Have you been here before?" she asked.

"No, but I have family who have. And they highly recommended it. Our villa is secluded so no one will here you scream," he said.

Sarah knew he was flirting, but the tone in his voice was almost sinister. She began to question her decision coming here with a man she barely knew.

"Then after, there are so many restaurants near the hotel that are on the beach. So we can watch the sunset while we eat dinner," he said.

The thought of dining on the beach at sunset erased Sarah's doubts.

"Oh wow. That will be beautiful," she said, trying to stay engaged in the conversation.

Everything Luca was saying sounded perfect. The villa, a private infinity pool, dinner at sunset – but her thoughts kept going back to Tim. She knew it should be him there with her. She tried to push him out of her head. It was only a few more days with Luca and then they could go their separate ways.

"How long are you staying here?" she asked.

"We have the villa for three nights," he replied.

Three nights. She could do that, she decided.

"Perfect," she said.

The baggage carousel started humming as it came to life. A few moments later, their luggage appeared.

Luca lifted their suitcases off the carousel and wheeled them to the exit. He hailed a cab and gave the driver the address to the hotel. It was about an hour drive from the airport to the hotel. Sarah fell asleep on the drive, with her head resting on Luca's shoulder. He gently woke her up when they arrived.

"Sarah, we're here," he said quietly.

She slowly opened her eyes and looked around. The resort was tucked away into its own private hillside, with the different villas spaced a part for privacy. They all overlooked the sea; which Sarah could see a glimpse of between the buildings. It was a beautiful turquoise color and reminded her of the Caribbean, but the water was calm.

The taxi driver exited the car and set their luggage on the walkway leading up to the resort. Luca went to pay the taxi driver, but Sarah interfered.

"No, I got it. You've paid for everything else so far," she said.

She quickly paid the driver before Luca could hesitate and walked toward their luggage. Luca quickly followed.

"You didn't have to do that," he said angrily.

"I know I didn't have to. But I feel bad. You've literally paid for everything – our rooms, the food," she said.

"It's not a big deal. It's just money, and I like spending my money on beautiful things," he said.

She let out a light laugh but felt slightly uncomfortable as if he thought he could buy her. Then he grabbed her hands and pulled her in close to him. He leaned his head down and kissed her passionately on the lips. It was a long, slow kiss. Sarah's thoughts had been erased. She wasn't thinking about the money comment or Tim. All she could think about was getting Luca to their room.

When they finally arrived to their room, it was the most beautiful hotel room Sarah had ever stayed in. Everything inside was so white and clean. The main entrance to the villa opened up to a living room area with all white furniture. To the side of that room was a kitchen and dining area. But once you walked through the living room, you walked down a hallway that led to the bedroom. Inside, there was a king-sized bed with all white linens. The bedroom was connected to the bathroom, which had a giant, white soaking tub that could easily fit two people. There was also a rain shower, a double vanity with two sinks, and of course – a toilet.

The bedroom and bathroom both had sliding glass doors that led to a deck outside. The deck was narrow, but led to their own, private infinity pool that overlooked the Andaman Sea. To the right of the pool was a canopy tent with two lounge chairs inside. The white curtains were pulled back and tied around the stands.

"What do you think?" Luca asked after they finished touring the place.

"This is unbelievable," Sarah replied.

She turned to look at him.

"This place can't be cheap. Please let me help pay for it," she offered, knowing she didn't have enough money to pay for a hotel like this.

"Signora, your money is no good here. Just let me take care of it. Besides, I already paid for this room before I saw you at the airport. So no, I cannot take your money," he said.

Your money is no good here, she repeated in her head. Something was different about him and she didn't like it. Then he walked toward her and held her hands.

"Please just enjoy it," he said.

She forced a smile.

"I will," she said.

"Good," he said as he picked her up in his arms and carried her into the bedroom.

"What are you doing?" she asked nervously.

"I'm going to enjoy you," he said excitedly.

Sarah wasn't in the mood. She didn't want to have sex with Luca, but she was almost scared to interject. So she just let it happen. After he fucked her, Luca went to rinse off in the shower. Sarah laid in bed feeling violated and used. She enjoyed having sex with him, but it felt different now. She felt like he saw her as a possession, and she didn't know why. She couldn't explain it to herself. She just felt weird.

She pushed those thoughts out of her head and walked outside naked. The trees surrounding their villa gave them enough privacy where the other guests couldn't see them. The smell of salt rang through the air and a light breeze brushed against her naked body. It felt freeing to Sarah. She spread her arms out into a stretch and looked out toward the sea. She could get used to this, she decided.

She walked toward the pool and dipped her toes in. The water was warm and inviting, almost like a bath. She slowly walked down the steps as the water surrounded her. The water was only about 4-feet deep and rested just under her breasts. She walked toward the edge of the pool and rested her arms on the ledge.

She looked down and saw how high up they were. If she were to fall, she would definitely die. She decided not to think about that. Instead, she looked straight out toward the sea. She was lost in her own thoughts she didn't even hear Luca wade into the pool behind her. She felt someone's arms wrap around her from behind and it caused her to jump.

"It's just me," he said calmingly.

"I didn't hear you come in. You scared me," she said nervously.

"You don't have to be scared. There's no one else around. It's just us," he said as he situated himself behind her.

No one else around, she repeated in her head. If she were to scream, no one would hear her. She suddenly realized the potential danger she could be in. She didn't want to stay there anymore. She wanted to leave. Something in Luca had changed and she no longer enjoyed his company.

Suddenly, she felt his nakedness. He had her front pressed against the ledge of the pool with his arms holding her there. She felt trapped. He leaned his head down and gently kissed her neck.

"Luca, please," she protested.

"Signora, don't fight it. You're mine now," he said.

He moved one of his hands from the ledge and firmly grabbed her breast. Her breathing accelerated. She knew what was about to happen, but she didn't want it to. For some reason, she couldn't speak. She just stood there frozen.

He slid his hand down her body and between her legs. He forced two fingers inside her aggressively. She let out a painful cry. His fingers were thick, and he was not being gentle as he had in the past. He pushed them into her harder and she felt pain. She wanted to cry out "stop," but she couldn't. She was frozen.

She could feel his penis growing hard against the back of her thigh. Then, just as quickly as his fingers entered her, he had removed them. He forced himself into her from behind and she was filled with more pain than she had ever felt in her entire life. She cried out.

"Yes," he moaned into her ear.

She wanted to cry. She wanted him to stop. But she couldn't speak. She couldn't move. She was frozen. So she stood there and waited for it to be over. But he continued to thrust into her as he grunted. After what felt like an eternity, she felt him relax against her back. Then he pulled himself out of her and patted her on the back.

"Good girl. Now don't try to leave because I will find you," he said threateningly before leaving the pool.

She heard the sliding glass door close, but she still couldn't move. She knew he finished inside her. She knew she had to get to a pharmacy to get a pill to prevent an unwanted pregnancy. She knew she had to get away from him. But she couldn't think. She couldn't move. She stayed there frozen.

She didn't know how much time had passed, but eventually she regained feeling of her legs. She slowly turned toward the villa. The sun was reflecting off the glass doors, so she couldn't see inside. But she knew she had to move. She couldn't stay in the pool forever. She walked out of the pool and became fully aware of the pain between her legs. She wanted to lay down and cry, but she knew she couldn't. She had to escape.

She slowly opened the door leading into the bathroom. She felt something wet between her legs and placed her hand there. She looked down at her fingers and saw blood. She rushed to the toilet and went to the bathroom – more blood. She kept wiping with toilet paper, but it hurt so bad and the blood seemed endless. It wasn't heavy like a period, but it was present.

She slowly walked to the sink and quietly turned it on just enough to wash her hands. Then she tiptoed to the doorway leading to the bedroom and peered slowly around the corner. Luca was lying in the bed asleep. She quietly entered the room and slowly dragged her luggage into the living room. She rummaged through her suitcase for some clothes and threw them on in a hurry.

She didn't look in a mirror. She didn't care how she looked. She didn't care that her hair was probably all over the place. She didn't know how much time she had before Luca woke up and she knew she had to run. She grabbed her suitcase and quietly left the villa. She ran down the paved pathway, up the hill toward the resort's main lobby. Once she got there, there were a few taxis waiting outside.

She got inside the closest one and asked the driver to take her to the airport. She had only been in Phuket a few hours, and she was ready to leave. She didn't want to go to a separate hotel. She didn't want to go somewhere where he might find her. *I will find you*, she heard him say in her head. She didn't even want to be in the same country as him. She wanted to get away from him.

During the hour drive back to the airport, Sarah booked the next available flight to the United States on her cell phone. She was ending her trip early and going home to Muncie. She didn't care how much the flight would cost her. She needed to get out of Thailand. And the only place she wanted to be was home.

Once she got to the airport and checked in, she had two hours before her flight left. She was terrified Luca was going to show up any minute. She kept looking over her shoulder expecting to see him, but he wasn't there. Then she remembered the pill! She walked up to a map of the airport and located a pharmacy.

She went inside the store and asked them if they sold anything that would help prevent an unplanned pregnancy. They told her yes and handed her a box that she couldn't read. All of the instructions were in Thai. She had to trust the pharmacist that this would work. She bought the box and a bottle of water. She exited the store and went and sat down on a bench. She quickly tore the box open, which revealed a single pill. She popped it into her mouth and swallowed it with a swig of water.

Even though she didn't believe in God, she prayed this would work. She didn't want to get pregnant. She didn't want to carry Luca's baby. Especially, not from a rape. Was it rape, she asked herself. She never told him no or to stop, she thought. She felt stupid. She should have intervened. She should have said something, she told herself.

She wanted to cry, but she was in public. She wasn't going to do that here. She wasn't going to give him the satisfaction of breaking her. He didn't break her. She was stronger than this. She was going to survive this, just as she had survived everything else this year had thrown at her.

    She stood up from the bench and walked to her gate. An hour later, she was on the plane. She still feared she was going to see Luca show up and drag her off the plane. But then the door closed, and the plane began to reverse. Once the tires lifted off the ground, she felt a sense of relief. She was no longer in Thailand and he could never hurt her again.

18

About 38 hours after leaving Thailand, Sarah arrived at the Indianapolis International Airport. Tim was going to meet her at baggage claim and drive her home to Muncie. She knew she was going to be too exhausted to drive herself home, so she called him during one of her layovers. He was confused she was coming home so early, but he was ecstatic to pick her up and see her.

She didn't tell him the reason her trip ended early. She felt guilty about spending her trip with Luca, and she didn't want Tim to think differently of her. She knew she should probably tell him at some point, but that wasn't going to be today, she decided. She exited the plane and followed the signs to the baggage claim area.

She saw Tim standing next to the carousel with a bouquet of calla lilies. When she saw him, it was like the weight of the world lifted from her shoulders. She felt relieved, safe, and maybe even a little happy. She ran into his arms and hugged him tighter than she ever hugged anyone. He wrapped his arms around her and hugged her equally as tight. He kissed the top of her head. And she started crying into his shoulder. He pulled back and looked at her face.

"Is everything OK?" he asked.

"It is now," she said, pulling him back into a hug.

He didn't say anything else. He just held her.

"I missed you so much," she said.

"I missed you too," he replied.

"I thought about you everywhere. It should have been you on that trip with me. We were supposed to go to Thailand together," she said.

"We were?" he asked confused.

She pulled away from the hug and looked up at him.

"I mean, ever since our first date I kind of pictured us going there together," she said.

"Ah. I see," he said smiling. "Next time."

"No," she said. "I don't want to go back."

Thailand had forever been ruined for her. She hated Luca for that. Thailand was her dream trip, and he spoiled the entire country for her. She knew she would never be able to return.

"Really?" he asked.

Before Sarah could respond, the carousel came to life. She moved closer so she could spot her luggage.

"I can grab it. Just let me know which one is yours," Tim said, following her.

"Thank you," she said, keeping an eye on the carousel.

"Before I forget, these are for you," he said, handing her the flowers.

"Thank you," she said, smiling at him.

Then she turned her attention back to the carousel.

"It's that black one," she said, pointing to a large, black suitcase coming their way.

Tim leaned over and lifted it off the carousel.

"That's heavy," he said.

"Yeah. I don't know how to pack light," she laughed.

He grabbed the handle with one hand and grabbed Sarah's hand with his other.

"Are you ready to go home?" he asked.

"More than anything," she replied, giving his hand a squeeze.

The hour drive to Muncie was quiet. Tim could sense Sarah didn't want to talk about her trip and he didn't want to press her. So instead, he turned on the radio and quietly sang along. Sarah held his hand and looked out the window. It felt good to be home, she thought.

They pulled into Sarah's driveway and the house looked just as she had left it. She had only been gone a little over a week, but it felt like so much longer to her. She wondered if it felt longer to Tim too. She missed him so much. He carried her luggage inside and stood by the door.

"You're probably exhausted from the long flight, so I'll let you get some rest. But call me tomorrow if you're up for it and we can do something," he said.

"You're leaving?" she asked sadly.

"I figured you would want to rest," he said. "I can stay if you want me to."

"Will you spend the night with me?" she asked.

"If you want me to," he answered.

"Yes, please," she said.

"OK," he said.

He grabbed her and pulled her into a hug. She pulled back and looked into his eyes.

"I love you, Tim," she said.

His lips curled up into a smile.

"What did you say?" he asked.

She smiled.

"I said, I love you," she replied.

"You have no idea how long I have waited to hear you say those words," he said.

He leaned down and kissed her softly on the lips. When he pulled away, she was smiling at him.

"I think I've known for a while, but this trip really made me realize how much you mean to me. And I don't ever want to let that go again," she said.

"Good," he said. "Because I don't think I could handle losing you twice."

Sarah hugged him close. But then she became aware of her smell and realized it had been two days since she last showered. She quickly stepped away from Tim and gave him a half-smile.

"I'm going to take a shower to get this travel smell off of me. In the meantime, you can make yourself at home," she said.

He laughed.

"Sounds good," he replied.

Sarah started sorting through her suitcase to find her bathroom essentials, but Tim stepped in.

"I can just carry that upstairs for you if you'd like," he offered.

"Yes, please," she said with a smile.

He carried the suitcase up the steps and set it outside the bathroom door.

"I'll be in your bedroom if you need anything," he said.

"Thank you," she replied.

He went into her bedroom and laid down on the bed. Sarah grabbed what she needed and went into the bathroom. She turned the shower on and stepped inside. As the water poured over her naked body, she was transported back to the pool in Phuket. The image of Luca ramming into her from behind would not leave her mind. It became hard for her to breathe and she thought she might be having a panic attack.

She focused on her breathing to get her heartrate back on track. Then she sat on the bottom of the tub, curled up into a ball, and cried. Even though she got away from him and would never see him again, she could not wash away the feeling it left behind. She felt violated, unworthy, and somehow like it was her fault. But she knew it wasn't.

She didn't do anything to provoke it. She wasn't even sure why it happened. She had willingly had sex with him so many times prior to that and probably would have again if that didn't happen. She was confused and hurt. The physical pain had diminished, but the emotional pain was very present.

She pulled herself back up and continued her shower. Once she turned the water off, the images of Luca disappeared. She wondered if every shower was going to remind her of that incident. She wondered if she would ever be able to enjoy a pool again. Probably not, she decided. He had ruined that for her.

She dried off with a towel and brushed her wet hair back and out of her face. Then she wrapped the towel around her body and walked into her bedroom to get dressed. She found Tim lying on her bed with his eyes closed. Sarah thought he might be sleeping, but he opened his eyes the second he heard her enter the room.

"Well, hello there," he said with a smile.

"Hello," she said laughing. "I came to get some clean clothes."

"You don't have to do that," he said.

He climbed off the bed and made his way toward Sarah. She took a step back as he approached her. He stopped and looked at her confused.

"I'm sorry. I thought you intentionally came in here naked. Um, I'll go sit back on your bed," he said as he turned around and went back to her bed.

She felt embarrassed. She didn't know why she took a step back. She knew Tim wasn't Luca. She knew he would never do to her what Luca did. Tim cared for her. He loved her. She knew that, but she couldn't fathom the thought of being touched by another man right now. She started crying. Tim turned back around and rushed to her. He wrapped his arms around her back and pulled her in close.

"Is everything OK?" he asked.

"No," she replied.

She hugged him back, letting the towel drop to the floor. She was fully aware she was naked, but she didn't care. She knew she was vulnerable, but she felt safe in Tim's arms. He picked her up and carried her to the bed, where he sat down on the edge and held her in his lap.

He could sense something happened on her trip, but he didn't want to pry. He knew she would tell him when she was ready. So he just held her. He didn't ask any questions. After what felt like a half hour, but was really only a couple minutes, Sarah stopped crying. She looked up at Tim.

"I was raped," she said.

Her voice quivered as she said the words out loud.

"What?" Tim asked angrily.

The tone in his voice scared her. She thought he was angry with her. She went to climb off his lap, but he held her close.

"Are you OK?" he asked concerningly.

"I don't know," she answered truthfully.

"I don't know what to say," he replied.

"It might not have been rape," she confessed.

"What do you mean?" he asked confused.

"I didn't say no or ask him to stop. I couldn't. I was frozen. My voice wouldn't work," she said.

Tim grabbed Sarah's face softly with his hand and forced her to look at him.

"This isn't your fault, Sarah. You know that, right?" he asked.

"But maybe if I had said something, this wouldn't have happened," she replied.

"I wasn't there, so I don't know all of the circumstances. But I know this wasn't your fault. And you need to know that too," he said.

"OK," she said.

"I am so sorry this happened to you," he said, holding her close to his chest.

Sarah suddenly became aware of her nakedness and shivered slightly.

"I'll get you some warm pajamas. You just stay here," Tim said as he gently placed her on the bed.

She pulled the blankets over her as he went to her dresser drawer and pulled out some fleece pajamas for her to wear. He walked back toward the bed and handed them to her.

"Thank you," she said as she got dressed.

"Anything you need, I am here. Anything at all," he said.

She leaned toward him and planted a kiss right on his lips.

"I appreciate you," she said.

"And I am so proud of you," he said as he took a seat next to her on the bed.

Sarah looked at him quizzically.

"Proud of me?" she asked confused.

"I know it wasn't easy telling me that. That took a lot of strength and courage to tell me. And you are one hell of a resilient woman, Sarah. I am so proud of you for everything you've conquered this year. You have no idea how proud of you I am," he said.

Resilient. Her aunt's words echoed in her head: *Us Simmons women are strong and resilient.* Aunt Susan, she thought.

"Remind me to call Aunt Susan tomorrow," she said.

"That's a weird topic change, but OK," Tim said with a smile.

Sarah smiled back. The thoughts of Luca vandalizing her began to go away.

"Something you said reminded me of something she said when we said goodbye," she said.

"How did that go anyway?" he asked.

"Oh my gosh, Tim. It was like something straight out of a movie. We showed up and he was standing there with dozens and dozens of red roses. He said there was one for every year he has been in love with her. It was the cutest thing ever. And his house was absolutely breathtaking," she said.

"That's good! So Susan seemed happy?" he asked.

"So happy. I'm glad I got to be there for that," she said.

"So when is she coming back?" he asked.

"She's not," Sarah replied sadly.

"I see," he said understandingly.

"They have already spent so much time a part. Now it's time for them to be together," she said.

"I get it. I still can't believe they kept in touch all of these years," Tim said.

"I know. It's crazy, but kind of romantic," she said.

"Don't make me be away from you for 40 years, OK?" he asked.

"Deal," she replied.

She leaned toward him and kissed him again. She let her lips linger on his for a moment before she pulled away.

"I've missed your kisses," she said.

"I've missed everything about you," he replied.

She smiled at him.

"But before we start this, there's something I need to know," he said seriously.

"What's that?" she asked concerned.

She was afraid he was going to ask about Thailand and how that even happened in the first place.

"Are you ready for this? Your divorce isn't even finalized yet and that's still fresh. If you need more time, I get it. I can wait. I would rather us wait then jump into something only to have you change your mind down the road," he said.

"Tim," she said, grabbing his hands. "I have never been more ready for anything in my life. I know what I want now. I didn't before. I was confused before. But I'm not anymore. I want you. I've always wanted you. I see that now," she said.

"And you're sure?" he asked.

"I am positive," she said.

19

Sarah woke up to an empty bed the next morning. The smell of bacon wafted through the air. She followed the smell down the stairs to the kitchen, where Tim was standing in a pair of black boxer briefs in front of the stove. He turned around as he heard her enter.

"Good morning," he said with a smile. "I figured you would be hungry so I'm making bacon and eggs."

"My favorite," she replied.

She took a seat at the table and spotted an envelope with her name on it.

"What's this?" she asked.

"I don't know. It was there when I came down here," he answered.

Sarah opened the envelope and recognized her aunt's handwriting.

"It's a letter from Aunt Susan," she said as she began to read.

"Oh, don't forget to call her later," he said.

But Sarah was preoccupied reading the letter to understand what he said.

Sarah,

As I write this letter, I know you're going to be mad at me for not telling you in person. But I knew if I did, you wouldn't have gone on that trip with me. You would have made me stay home while you took care of me. And I just couldn't have that. I needed to see Chun-chieh before I die. Yes, die. You read that correctly.

I was recently diagnosed with cancer. It's not good. They told me I don't have long to live, and it has metastasized to other parts of my body. There isn't anything they can do to slow it down. I have accepted my time has come, and I hope you will too. I know this will not be easy for you to hear, or read rather, but you are strong, and you will get through this. I know you will.

And I want you to know visiting Chun was my dying wish. I knew there was a chance this trip would kill me, but it was a risk I was willing to take. Chun is my one true love and I had to see him, even if only for a moment, before I leave this world behind. So I hope you find peace in knowing I was happy in my final moments and surrounded by the man for whom my heart has longed for far too long.

Thank you for taking this trip with me. I would not have been able to do it without you. I hope you enjoyed your time in Thailand and found what you were looking for. You are a beautiful, wonderful woman; and anyone would be lucky to be able to call you theirs. I truly hope you find your happiness.

Love always,
Aunt Susan

Sarah looked up from the letter and realized she was crying. She had no idea her aunt was sick. How could she not have noticed, she thought. She saw the way the disease had weakened her father. Looking back, she saw the same symptoms in her aunt. She had been fatigued lately and had moments of confusion. But Sarah wasn't paying attention. She was too preoccupied with her own problems.

If she paid closer attention, maybe there was something she could have done, she thought. Then she realized there wasn't. Cancer was a bitch, and it didn't wait for anyone. Sarah placed the letter down and wiped her tears away. She ran upstairs and grabbed her cell phone. Standing in the middle of her bedroom, she called her aunt.

"Hello?" a man's voice said after a few rings.

"Chun-chieh?" Sarah asked.

"Yes. Sarah?" he replied.

"Yes, this is Sarah. Chun, is my aunt around?" she asked in a panic.

There was silence.

"I wanted to call you, Sarah. But she told me not to. She wanted you to enjoy your trip. She said it was something you needed to do," he said.

Sarah began to cry again.

"Is she there?" she asked again.

"She died three days after you left," he said quietly.

Sarah began to backtrack her trip. Three days after leaving Taiwan she would have been … in Phuket. Her mouth hung open as she pictured her aunt dropping dead the moment Luca was violating her. Her whole body began to shake.

"Sarah?" Chun-chieh asked.

She realized she hadn't said anything in a moment.

"I'm here," she said.

"She knew her time had come. She had accepted it. And I want you to know, in her final moments, she was truly happy. She told me that. I love her more than I have ever loved anyone, and that has helped me find peace during this time. I hope it will help you as well," he said calmly.

"Thank you, Chun-chieh," she said. "And thank you for being there for her when it happened. I am happy she had you in her life."

"It was my honor. And Sarah, if you ever need anything or just want someone to talk to, I am here," he said.

"I appreciate that, Chun-chieh. Thank you," she said.

"And one more thing. Suzie left you her house and all of her assets. She said all of the information you will need is in her desk drawer," he said.

She was speechless. She didn't know what to say. She realized she was her aunt's only family, but she wasn't expecting this.

"Are you still there, Sarah?" Chun-chieh asked.

"I'm still here. I just, I don't know what to say," she replied.

"You don't have to say anything. I know this is a lot to process. But as I said, I am here if you need anything," he said.

"Thank you, Chun-chieh. We'll talk soon," she said.

"I look forward to it. Goodbye, Sarah," he said.

"Goodbye, Chun-chieh," she said.

She ended the phone call and stared blankly at her cell phone screen. Her aunt, her only living relative, was now dead. And she didn't even see it coming. She had no idea. She should have suspected something when her aunt said she wanted to go to Asia, but she didn't. She was too preoccupied with her own life. She knew nothing would have changed the outcome. Susan went exactly how she wanted to, near the love of her life. That gave Sarah a little sense of peace, but she was still astonished. She looked up and saw Tim standing in the doorway. She didn't even hear him come up the stairs.

"Is everything OK?" he asked.

"She's dead," she replied.

"Who's dead? Susan?" he asked concerned.

Sarah nodded her head yes.

"Oh my gosh, Sarah. I am so sorry. What happened?" he asked as he rushed across the room to hold her.

"Cancer," she answered.

Tim didn't know what to say. Instead, he just held her in silence.

"I should have known something was up. But I didn't. I didn't pay attention. I was too preoccupied with my own, stupid problems," she said as she pulled away from his hug.

"Sarah, stop. First of all, your problems are not stupid. You have been through a lot this year. More than most people. Secondly, there's nothing you could have done. Cancer is a tricky disease. And sometimes, there just isn't anything you can do," he said.

She knew everything he was saying was correct, but it didn't change the way she felt. She tried to think back to what Chun-chieh had said - *in her final moments, she was truly happy. She told me that.*

"At least she was happy," she said.

Tim looked at her confused.

"She knew she was dying, and she wanted to see the love of her life before she went. Even if just for a moment. I'm happy I was able to make that happen for her. Because of that, she died happy," she said.

"Are you OK?" he asked.

"I don't know," she replied.

"You're probably not hungry now, but if you are, breakfast is done," he said with half a smile.

"Surprisingly, I think I can eat," she said.

Tim led her downstairs, holding her hand. They sat at the kitchen table and ate their breakfast in silence. Sarah looked around the room and imagined her dad and Susan sitting at the table with them. She could hear her dad cracking an inappropriate joke and Susan glancing at him across the room while Tim laughed.

Her dad would have approved of Tim, she thought. She knew he met him, and mentioned him in his letter before he died, but now, all of this time later, she knew she made the right decision. Tim was her Chun. It just didn't take 40 years of being a part to realize it. And for that, she was thankful.

A part of her heart will always ache for what she did to Charlie, but she knew she didn't love him the way he loved her. And they both deserved better. She hoped with all of her heart he would find that one day. He deserved that. He deserved to be happy the way Susan was with Chun. The way she was with Tim.

In the meantime, she was going to enjoy taking things slow with Tim. Too much had happened in the time they were a part to jump right back into things. She wanted to do things right this time. She was going to enjoy watching their love grow and bloom into something more beautiful than she could ever imagine. She looked across the table at him.

"I love you," she said.

"I love you, too," he replied.

Growing Love

Brianna Owczarzak

FROM THE AUTHOR

Thank you so much for reading my *Tangled Love* series. If you enjoyed it, please visit the website you purchased it from and leave a short review. Your feedback means a lot to me and will help other readers determine if this book is right for them.

If you would like to be notified of new releases, please follow me on Facebook, Instagram and Twitter by searching for Brianna Owczarzak.

Brianna Owczarzak

ABOUT THE AUTHOR

Brianna Owczarzak is a digital journalist and novelist. She has a B.S. in journalism from Central Michigan University (fire up chips) and an AAA from Delta College. Aside from writing, Brianna enjoys bankrupting her friends and family in Monopoly, and traveling the world. She lives in Michigan with her dog, Edgar Allan Paw.

Made in the USA
Columbia, SC
20 April 2022